A CHANCE CHRISTMAS

(THE INN AT DUNE ISLAND—BOOK 4)

FIONA GRACE

Fiona Grace

Fiona Grace is author of the LACEY DOYLE COZY MYSTERY series, comprising nine books; of the TUSCAN VINEYARD COZY MYSTERY series, comprising seven books; of the DUBIOUS WITCH COZY MYSTERY series, comprising three books; of the BEACHFRONT BAKERY COZY MYSTERY series, comprising six books; of the CATS AND DOGS COZY MYSTERY series, comprising nine books; of the ELIZA MONTAGU COZY MYSTERY series, comprising nine books (and counting); of the ENDLESS HARBOR ROMANTIC COMEDY series, comprising nine books (and counting); of the INN AT DUNE ISLAND ROMANTIC COMEDY series, comprising five books (and counting); of the INN BY THE SEA ROMANTIC COMEDY series, comprising five books (and counting); and of the MAID AND THE MANSION COZY MYSTERY series, comprising five books (and counting).

Fiona would love to hear from you, so please visit www.fionagraceauthor.com to receive free ebooks, hear the latest news, and stay in touch.

ISBN: 978-1-0943-8470-2

BOOKS BY FIONA GRACE

THE MAID AND THE MANSION COZY MYSTERY

A MYSTERIOUS MURDER (Book #1)
A SCANDALOUS DEATH (Book #2)
A MISSING GUEST (Book #3)
AN UNSOLVABLE CRIME (Book #4)
AN IMPOSSIBLE HEIST (Book #5)

INN BY THE SEA ROMANTIC COMEDY

A NEW LOVE (Book #1)
A NEW CHANCE (Book #2)
A NEW HOME (Book #3)
A NEW LIFE (Book #4)
A NEW ME (Book #5)

THE INN AT DUNE ISLAND ROMANTIC COMEDY

A CHANCE LOVE (Book #1)
A CHANCE FALL (Book #2)
A CHANCE ROMANCE (Book #3)
A CHANCE CHRISTMAS (Book #4)
A CHANCE ENGAGEMENT (Book #5)

ENDLESS HARBOR ROMANTIC COMEDY

ALWAYS, WITH YOU (Book #1)
ALWAYS, FOREVER (Book #2)
ALWAYS, PLUS ONE (Book #3)
ALWAYS, TOGETHER (Book #4)
ALWAYS, LIKE THIS (Book #5)
ALWAYS, FATED (Book #6)
ALWAYS, FOR LOVE (Book #7)
ALWAYS, JUST US (Book #8)
ALWAYS, IN LOVE (Book #9)

ELIZA MONTAGU COZY MYSTERY

MURDER AT THE HEDGEROW (Book #1)
A DALLOP OF DEATH (Book #2)
CALAMITY AT THE BALL (Book #3)

A SPEAKEASY DEMISE (Book #4)
A FLAPPER FATALITY (Book #5)
BUMPED BY A DAME (Book #6)
A DOLL'S DEBACLE (Book #7)
A FELLA'S RUIN (Book #8)
A GAL'S OFFING (Book #9)

LACEY DOYLE COZY MYSTERY
MURDER IN THE MANOR (Book#1)
DEATH AND A DOG (Book #2)
CRIME IN THE CAFE (Book #3)
VEXED ON A VISIT (Book #4)
KILLED WITH A KISS (Book #5)
PERISHED BY A PAINTING (Book #6)
SILENCED BY A SPELL (Book #7)
FRAMED BY A FORGERY (Book #8)
CATASTROPHE IN A CLOISTER (Book #9)

TUSCAN VINEYARD COZY MYSTERY
AGED FOR MURDER (Book #1)
AGED FOR DEATH (Book #2)
AGED FOR MAYHEM (Book #3)
AGED FOR SEDUCTION (Book #4)
AGED FOR VENGEANCE (Book #5)
AGED FOR ACRIMONY (Book #6)
AGED FOR MALICE (Book #7)

DUBIOUS WITCH COZY MYSTERY
SKEPTIC IN SALEM: AN EPISODE OF MURDER (Book #1)
SKEPTIC IN SALEM: AN EPISODE OF CRIME (Book #2)
SKEPTIC IN SALEM: AN EPISODE OF DEATH (Book #3)

BEACHFRONT BAKERY COZY MYSTERY
BEACHFRONT BAKERY: A KILLER CUPCAKE (Book #1)
BEACHFRONT BAKERY: A MURDEROUS MACARON (Book #2)
BEACHFRONT BAKERY: A PERILOUS CAKE POP (Book #3)
BEACHFRONT BAKERY: A DEADLY DANISH (Book #4)
BEACHFRONT BAKERY: A TREACHEROUS TART (Book #5)
BEACHFRONT BAKERY: A CALAMITOUS COOKIE (Book #6)

CATS AND DOGS COZY MYSTERY

A VILLA IN SICILY: OLIVE OIL AND MURDER (Book #1)
A VILLA IN SICILY: FIGS AND A CADAVER (Book #2)
A VILLA IN SICILY: VINO AND DEATH (Book #3)
A VILLA IN SICILY: CAPERS AND CALAMITY (Book #4)
A VILLA IN SICILY: ORANGE GROVES AND VENGEANCE (Book #5)
A VILLA IN SICILY: CANNOLI AND A CASUALTY (Book #6)

CHAPTER ONE

April stood by the dining room window, cradling a steaming cup of coffee in her hands as she gazed out at the ranch property that stretched before her. The morning sunlight cast a golden hue on the rolling hills, dotted with trees and fenced pastures.

Her house, once a place filled with childhood memories, had been lovingly transformed into a cozy bed and breakfast for tourists visiting the island.

Taking a slow sip of her rich, dark coffee, April allowed herself a brief moment of respite from the seemingly endless list of tasks demanding her attention. Thanksgiving had come and gone in the blink of an eye, and Christmas was fast approaching – only two short weeks away.

Her mind turned to everything she needed to get done: putting up Christmas decorations, buying gifts for friends and family, and ensuring the bed and breakfast was prepared for the influx of holiday guests. She took another sip of her coffee and sighed, knowing there was no time to waste.

She watched the horses run around the newly built pasture. It was large enough to hold the ten horses she'd been able to save from Isaac so far.

He'd tried to take the native horses from the island, but April was a fighter. It was a long, tense battle. But she had come out on top. At least until the courts decided if she was allowed to become a national nature reserve.

And who knew how long that would take?

She took in a deep breath and watched the playful horses run past the water basins and into the field of grass to snack on the foliage. It felt good to know that she was part of the reason the horses were able to stay on the island.

It felt even better that the horses were enjoying their time on the property so far. Though it was difficult to start adjusting their schedules and get them accustomed to the ranch lifestyle, it was worth it to see them happy and healthy.

Eventually, they would all be broken to become therapy horses for the people and visitors of the Sandcrest. But for now, it was one day at a time.

Setting her cup down on the windowsill, April strode through the dining room. The smell of freshly baked muffins lingered in the air, mingling with the scent of cinnamon and nutmeg.

A fire crackled merrily in the fireplace, casting flickering shadows on the walls covered with photographs of the surrounding island scenery.

"Morning, April!" Kristy greeted cheerfully from the lobby area where she was helping a couple check in. The new hire, with her enthusiasm and natural warmth, had quickly become irreplaceable to the bed and breakfast's daily operations.

"Good morning, Kristy," April replied with a smile, pausing briefly to watch as the young woman efficiently handled the guests' needs. It warmed her heart knowing that someone so capable and trustworthy was now part of her team.

That hadn't always been the case. When she first hired someone, they'd stolen from her. It was hard to trust again, but Kristy turned out to be the perfect fit for the place.

"April, do you know where the extra towels are?" Kristy asked, glancing over at her.

"Top shelf in the linen closet," April responded, resuming her walk into the lobby. As she passed Kristy and the guests, she thought about how busy she was despite the new hands to take over for her.

"Thanks, I'll grab them for our guests," Kristy said, beaming at April before disappearing down the hallway.

As April watched Kristy gather the towels, she couldn't help but feel a sense of relief wash over her. Through all the interviews and hiccups, she had finally found someone she trusted.

Taking a deep breath, April turned her attention back to the tasks at hand. There was much to do, and time was slipping away. She picked up her pace, knowing her little break had already set her daily schedule behind.

With Kristy taking care of the guests and managing the daily operations, it allowed April to focus more on the ranch and the horses, which was where her heart truly belonged.

The crisp winter air nipped at her cheeks as she stepped outside, making her way towards the barn. Her breath formed small puffs of white mist with each exhale. The snow-covered ground crunched beneath her boots, a stark contrast to the serene silence that enveloped the ranch.

"Hey there, you guys ready for breakfast?" April called out softly as she entered the barn. The horses greeted her with gentle whinnies. Only some of them were set up here, the others stayed out most of the day, wrapped in their winter gear and able to run about the field.

The others were inside for various reasons. Some needed rest for a leg injury, one wasn't accustomed to the ranch life yet and was trying to jump the fences when in the pasture, and one had been a little shy, needing more time to join the family.

She moved from stall to stall, inspecting the newly wrapped wounds with a practiced eye. It was hard to see on the excited feet of one, who pranced around its stall, waiting for the sweet pebbles of food to hit its bucket.

"Everything looks good so far," she thought, pleased by the progress the injured horses were making. The vet had been thorough in his instructions, and they had developed a solid plan to ensure the animals' comfort and recovery.

April went about her routine, mixing feed and putting it out to each eager horse. Their soft nickers and contented chewing filled the barn as she worked, bringing a smile to her face. These quiet moments with the horses were what made all the hard work worthwhile.

"Morning, Zeus," she whispered to the large chestnut stallion, running her hand affectionately along his strong neck. "How are you feeling today?"

Zeus responded with a nudge of his velvety muzzle against her palm, his dark eyes seeming to convey his gratitude. She felt a swell of pride, knowing that her dedication to the ranch and the horses was making a difference.

"Alright, I'll leave you to enjoy your breakfast," April said with a chuckle, patting Zeus one last time before closing his stall door.

As she completed her tasks, April's thoughts wandered back to the bed and breakfast, the guests, and Kristy. It was truly amazing how much had changed in such a short amount of time.

She allowed herself a moment to bask in the satisfaction of her accomplishments as she swept up the last of the hay and feed that had fallen to the barn floor.

Things are finally falling into place, she thought, grateful for all the support she had found in this small town.

And with Christmas just around the corner, she felt a sense of hope and excitement for what the future might hold.

As April moved on to the next stall, her thoughts drifted to Jackson, the quiet and kind ranch hand who had been a constant presence in both her life and the lives of the horses.

The memory of his light eyes and short, messy hair brought an involuntary smile to her face. She felt a pang of disappointment when she recalled his absence at Thanksgiving dinner.

"Morning, Orion," April greeted the gentle being, hiding her unease behind a warm smile. "You're looking better today."

He whinnied softly, nuzzling April's outstretched hand as he accepted a handful of feed. The stallion's trusting gaze only deepened April's sense of loss; it was Jackson who had first introduced them, and now he was nowhere to be found.

She wished Jackson had been here to help her with all of this. He knew more about horses than anyone in town. He'd been there to help her fight for the native animals, but then left without more than a note.

Unable to shake her concern, April sought solace in the familiar actions of caring for the horses. Each scoop of feed, each tender pat, seemed to offer a momentary reprieve from the gnawing worry that threatened to consume her.

She wondered if she'd done something to push him away. It was hard not to overthink every interaction trying to find some reason, some explanation to calm her worry.

Her mind raced through their past interactions, searching for any indication that she had made him uncomfortable or unwelcome. They had always been friendly, even flirtatious at times, but nothing that would warrant such a hasty departure.

Though the uncertainty still loomed over her, she thought about the chance that it wasn't about her. Maybe there was another reason he left.

But as much as she tried to reassure herself, April couldn't shake the nagging feeling that her growing affection for Jackson had played a role in his decision to leave. And with every passing day that he remained out of touch, her fear that he might never return grew stronger.

Silently, she pleaded with him to come back. Everything was hard enough. Without him, it was even harder.

April knew that he was always going to be in her corner. And she needed that right now. In the transition of working with the horses full time, she needed the reassurance and help right now.

Her plea echoed in her mind, unanswered except for the soft sounds of the horses munching on their breakfasts. And as April finished her chores, her heart ached with the weight of unresolved feelings and the longing for a future that seemed to be slipping through her fingers.

With the last of the hay distributed among the stalls, April stood back and wiped the sweat from her forehead with the back of her hand. She could feel the stinging bite of the cold air on her cheeks as it mingled with warm puffs of breath from the horses nearby. The scent of fresh hay and sweet feed filled her nostrils, grounding her in the moment.

"Alright, you guys enjoy your breakfast," she said softly, giving a gentle pat to the nose of a curious brown mare before stepping out of the stall.

As she walked towards the barn door, the rough wooden floorboards creaked beneath her boots, echoing through the quiet space.

April reached into her pocket and pulled out her phone, its screen casting a soft glow in the dimly lit barn. Her thumb hovered over the touch screen, hesitating for a beat before swiping to check her notifications.

"Nothing," she murmured, disappointment settling heavily in her chest. "Not even a text."

Her thoughts drifted to Jackson, and an involuntary sigh escaped her lips. She had only tried calling him once since he left two weeks ago, not wanting to intrude or seem desperate. But her heart longed for answers, for any hint of his well-being or intentions.

She thought about calling him again, her finger hovering over his contact. The call button seemed to mock her as she contemplated the decision. What if she was bothering him? What if he left because he wanted space? Who was she to intrude?

The uncertainty gnawed at her insides, twisting her stomach into knots. She shook her head as if to clear it from the doubts and fears.

April knew she couldn't call him again. If he wanted to talk, he'd have called her by now. It was time to give him space, even if it meant that she wouldn't know what was going on in his head.

Even if he wasn't going to come back, she should give him the space he clearly asked for.

With a heavy heart, she tucked her phone back into her pocket and stepped out of the barn, closing the door behind her. The crisp winter air enveloped her, its icy fingers reaching through the layers of her clothing and chilling her to the bone.

But even as she shivered, she enjoyed being outside in the fresh air. When she was cold, she didn't have to think about anything else. She could just look over the fields, watching the horses play and focus on the tasks at hand.

She wrapped her arms as she pulled a bucket of feed behind her to fill the pails in the pasture. The horses swarmed the fence line as she filled each one with a quarter of the filled bucket.

It was an uphill battle getting them to understand how to stick to their own feed, but some day she knew they would figure it out. Until then, she stood wrapped up in the cold, trying to ensure they stayed separated and got their fills.

When they were each done, they ran back into the field to graze again. April watched them play until she couldn't take the cold any longer.

As she trudged back towards the warm lights of the bed and breakfast, every step felt heavier than the last, burdened by the weight of heartache and unresolved feelings.

And as the distance between her and the barn grew, so too did the ache in her chest, a constant reminder of the budding interest in Jackson that seemed to be slipping further and further away with each passing day.

CHAPTER TWO

April stepped into the cozy warmth of the bed and breakfast, her cheeks flushed from the brisk winter air. She peeled off her gloves and shook the powdery snow from her dark hair. The scent of cinnamon and pine filled her nostrils as she hung her jacket on the rustic wooden coatrack.

"Mom!" Georgia's voice rang through the hallway, pulling April's attention towards her daughter. With her wavy long hair and green eyes, she was a spitting image of a young April. "You're back already!"

"Georgia!" April's face lit up at the sight of her daughter. She'd arrived a few days prior for her winter break from college. "I was thinking maybe we could watch one of those cheesy Christmas movies together until it's time to feed the horses again."

"Actually, Mom," Georgia hesitated, her fingers fidgeting with the strap of her purse. "I really need to grab some coffee from the shop. There's some stuff I have to get done. Would you like me to bring you some?"

"Of course, sweetheart. I'd love a coffee. Thank you," April replied, attempting to hide her disappointment. She had envisioned spending quality time with Georgia, who seemed to be constantly on the go since coming home from college.

Georgia pulled her jacket over her arms, slipping out her hair from under the hood. She was getting ready to leave just as April was getting ready to settle in. April couldn't say it didn't hurt to see her leave.

"Great! See you later then," Georgia said, leaning in to give April a quick peck on the cheek. April savored the moment, inhaling the familiar scent of her daughter's perfume.

"Have fun," April called out as Georgia slipped out the door, leaving her standing alone in the foyer.

April sighed, her breath fogging the window as she watched Georgia's retreating figure. The snow crunched beneath her daughter's boots, leaving trails of footprints that seemed to mirror the growing distance between them.

It wasn't just coffee runs and walks; it felt like Georgia was slipping away at every moment. The holiday was supposed to be bringing them together, but it seemed like every time April had a chance to spend time with her, she was leaving.

"Everything okay, April?" Kristy's voice pulled her back into the present moment. She glanced over at the young woman who had become a much-needed part of her life since starting work at the bed and breakfast.

"Sorry, I was just... thinking." April forced a smile, then settled into the chair next to Kristy behind the front desk.

The worn leather creaked under her weight as she leaned back, absently tapping a pen against the reservation book in front of her. "You're closer to Georgia's age, aren't you?"

"I mean, I'm a younger adult," Kristy replied, her eyes flicking up from the computer screen. "Why do you ask?"

"Christmas is coming up, and I'm trying to think of what to get her." April hesitated, feeling vulnerable as she admitted her uncertainty.

April had her eye on a heated blanket for the chilly dorm nights, or gift cards to local restaurants on campus. But none of it felt like it would be exciting enough for Georgia to receive.

April wanted to get her daughter something special. After everything they'd been through and everything Georgia had helped her with, she wanted to give something nice.

"I had a few ideas, but... I thought you might have a better idea."

"I'm sure you have great ideas," Kristy assured her, before pausing thoughtfully. "But maybe there's something personal that would show her how much she means to you?"

"Such as?" April prodded gently, hoping for inspiration.

"Something that represents your bond, or an inside joke only the two of you share," Kristy suggested, her almond-shaped eyes gleaming with enthusiasm. "That way, even when she's away at college, she'll always have a little piece of home with her."

"I'll have to think about that. I'm not sure if I have any ideas right now. We've had moments, but how do I pick something that will be important to her?" April asked, mostly thinking aloud.

April absently traced the edge of the book in front of her, her thoughts still lingering on Georgia. It was a challenge to find something meaningful for her daughter, who didn't have any particular collections or interests that could be easily translated into a gift.

She mentally sifted through memories of laughter and shared secrets, searching for that perfect gift. As she pondered, she couldn't help but feel grateful for Kristy's wisdom and the camaraderie they had developed. The young woman truly was a blessing in her life.

"Well, thanks anyway," April murmured, turning her attention back to the reservation book. She would find the right gift, something to impress Georgia. It just might take her more time than she had on hand.

"Actually," Kristy piped up, leaning in as if sharing a secret. "One year, my mom got me this little elephant figurine because they're my favorite animal. I absolutely loved it because every time I looked at it, I thought of her."

"An elephant figurine?" April repeated, a small smile tugging at her lips. She tried to picture Georgia's reaction to such a trinket, but it didn't quite fit her daughter's lack of trinkets.

"Of course, it doesn't have to be an elephant," Kristy laughed, her cheeks flushing with warmth. "It's just an example of how a simple, meaningful gift can mean so much more than something expensive or trendy."

"Thank you, Kristy," April said sincerely, her fingers tapping rhythmically against the receptionist desk. "I appreciate your input. It's given me something to think about."

"Anytime!" Kristy chirped, her eyes brightening. She seemed genuinely pleased to help.

"Speaking of which," April continued, turning her gaze to the young woman. "You've been such a wonderful addition to this place. Your hard work and dedication have made my life so much easier, and I'm grateful for that."

Kristy's cheeks flushed a deeper shade of pink, and she ducked her head, clearly touched by the compliment. "Thank you, April. I'm really glad I took this job. It's been a great experience, and I enjoy being here."

"Are you going to see your family for the holidays?" April asked, genuinely interested in Kristy's plans.

"Yes, I'll be seeing some family, some friends," Kristy replied, a soft smile playing on her lips. "It'll be nice to catch up with everyone. We have our own traditions, you know how it goes."

"Make sure to tell your mom she raised a thoughtful and insightful daughter," April said warmly. "I'm sure she'll appreciate hearing that."

"Thank you, April. I will," Kristy promised, her eyes shining with gratitude.

As they shared a moment of mutual appreciation, April felt a renewed sense of determination to find that perfect gift for Georgia –

one that would convey the depth of her love. She knew it wouldn't be easy, but with Kristy's help, it suddenly seemed possible.

The snowflakes danced in the air outside, painting a serene picture of winter's embrace, and April found herself momentarily transfixed by their grace. She sighed, her thoughts still preoccupied with finding the perfect gift for Georgia, when Kristy spoke up again.

"Hey, April, why don't you go out and do some shopping while we're waiting for the next meal? I'll keep an eye on things here, make sure none of the horses get into any trouble. I'll check on them, so you don't have to worry."

April hesitated, her gaze returning to the wintry scene beyond the window. The thought of leaving her beloved ranch while there was so much to do made her feel queasy.

It wasn't just the horses that needed to be fed and watched. The ranch needed to grow in order to begin work on the horses and build the sanctuary April had been envisioning.

But she knew she needed to find that special gift for Georgia. She was already behind in her shopping and Christmas preparation.

"Alright," she agreed, running her fingers through her dark hair. "I suppose I could use a break – and maybe inspiration will strike while I'm out."

"Exactly," Kristy encouraged, her eyes bright and reassuring. "And don't worry, I've got everything under control here. The horses will be fine."

"Thank you, Kristy," April said, smiling gratefully. As she pulled on her coat and gloves, she couldn't help but marvel at how lucky she was to have found such a reliable employee in this small town.

"Good luck!" Kristy called after her as April stepped out into the crisp December air, the door shutting behind her with a soft click.

The snow crunched beneath April's boots as she made her way towards the car. The wintry air nipped at her cheeks, a stark contrast to the warmth she felt inside the ranch.

She wrapped her coat tighter around herself, determined to find that perfect gift for Georgia, and made her way towards town.

CHAPTER THREE

The quaint island town shimmered like a snow globe under the moonlit sky, each building adorned with twinkling fairy lights that turned the streets into a picturesque wonderland. Shop windows showcased festive displays, enticing passersby to peer inside and admire the lovingly crafted local wares.

In the heart of the town square stood a magnificent Christmas tree, assembled by the locals with great care and dedication. Its branches, heavy with ornaments and gleaming baubles, reached out as if to embrace the community it represented.

Multicolored lights cascaded down from its peak, bathing the surrounding area in a warm, inviting glow. The sweet scent of pine mingled with the crisp winter air, creating a festive atmosphere that was hard to resist.

Despite the chilly weather, there were still some tourists visiting from out of state, their lack of jackets a clear sign they had underestimated the bite of the island's winter breeze. April wrapped her scarf tighter around her neck as she walked through town, taking in the familiar sights and sounds of the season.

"April! Fancy seeing you here," called Alice, her rosy cheeks peeking out from beneath a woolen hat. April's friend Alice's smile brought a sense of comfort and familiarity to the otherwise bustling and chaotic holiday season.

"Hey Alice!" April replied with a grin, embracing her friend warmly.

"How are you? Are you ready for the holidays?" Alice asked, with several bags swinging from her arms.

"Ready?" April let out a chuckle. "I've still got so much to do. My mantel looks like a disaster zone, and I haven't even gotten my tree yet."

"Tell me about it," Alice sighed, "I feel behind, too. It's coming up so fast!"

It felt like Alice had just finished all of her shopping, while April knew she would be lucky to get a few gifts out of today's trip to town. She felt so far behind where she wanted to be.

"Have you managed to decorate your place yet?" Alice asked, her eyes sparkling with curiosity. "I just bought some gorgeous garland for our railings on the stairs." She smiled, clearly overcome with holiday glee.

"Between running the ranch and trying to find gifts for everyone, I'm way behind on my decorating," April admitted, her shoulders sagging slightly under the weight of her holiday to-do list.

"Ah, don't worry about it!" Alice reassured her. "We've all been there. Besides, there's still some time left. You'll get it done."

"Thanks, Alice," April smiled, feeling a renewed sense of determination. "I know you're right, but sometimes it just feels like there aren't enough hours in the day, you know?"

"Of course," Alice agreed with a sympathetic nod. "But you've got this, April. Remember, it's not about the decorations or the presents – it's about spending time with the people we care about."

"True words." April nodded, feeling a warmth in her heart that had little to do with her cozy scarf.

It hurt to think about Georgia not being home much during this holiday season. It felt like she was always fighting to get time with her. Still, she knew that she had to do what she could to make Christmas as joyful as she could.

Feeling determined to accomplish something from her long to-do list, she continued her journey through the twinkling town. She was going to embrace the spirit of the season and enjoy whatever moments she got with her family and friends.

April walked through the streets of downtown, the cool sea breeze lifting her spirits as she took in the sights of the busy streets. The shops lining the cobblestone streets were full of people searching for gifts and decor to make the season special.

In the center of town, April stopped at the Christmas tree, tall and proud, with ornaments made by hand and stories behind each one. It was a symbol of unity and love in their close-knit community. She knew she would have to get a tree and some new ornaments, but this would bring up her spirits in the meantime.

She noticed a few tourists, easily identified by their lack of jackets, wandering among the locals with wide eyes and bright smiles. April remembered her first time visiting the island, filled with the same sense of wonder at its beauty.

Thinking of her conversation with Alice, April felt a pang of guilt, knowing that she hadn't picked up any gifts for her friends yet. She wondered if one of the bags Alice was holding held something special for her.

She didn't expect gifts in return, but she knew that she would feel awful not celebrating the friends that made life in town so much easier and much more fun.

As she continued walking, she came across the familiar sign for Giant's, the burger joint that Nigel owned. A wave of nostalgia washed over her as she thought about him and their breakup. They both knew they weren't working out, and while it was sad to lose something like that, it was for the best.

Sometimes things just don't work out, April thought, allowing herself a moment of vulnerability. After her divorce, she wasn't sure she'd find anyone else, but life in this small town had shown her that love could bloom again.

Her thoughts drifted to Jackson, her ranch hand, and how much she missed having him around. Her feelings had grown for him, despite the current distance between them. His kindness and mysterious nature had captured her attention, leaving her longing for his presence.

April knew there was still hope for her love life. Her heart swells with warmth at the thought of Jackson. The holiday season was a time for love and connection, and April was starting to believe that she could find both once again.

With that thought in mind, she stepped forward into the festive atmosphere of the town, ready to embrace the season and all it had to offer.

April entered the general store, her cheeks flushed from the chilly air outside. The warm, inviting atmosphere enveloped her as she glanced around at the neatly arranged shelves adorned with festive decorations.

She was immediately greeted by a familiar face, Chuck, who had an infectious smile and a thick southern accent that hadn't always made her feel welcome in this quaint island town.

When they'd first met, he and his friends had told April that she wasn't going to make it renovating her family home that had gotten into bad shape over the years. But thankfully, Chuck had become more open to the idea of her around town when she'd finished the house and had become a successful bed and breakfast.

"Hey there, April!" he called out, his eyes twinkling with holiday cheer. "Haven't seen you in quite some time. How's the bed and breakfast going?"

"Hi, Chuck! It's been going better than expected," she replied, winking at him. Her heart swelled with pride at the thought of her successful venture. "The house is finally starting to feel like home."

"Ah, of course," Chuck grinned, giving her a playful nudge. "I admit, me and the boys didn't think you'd be able to pull it off, but you proved us wrong. We're glad to have you here, April."

"Thanks, Chuck. That means a lot." She smiled warmly before remembering her current predicament.

"Speaking of home, are you all set for Christmas? It's just around the corner," he asked.

April sighed, rubbing the back of her neck as a tinge of stress crept into her expression. "To be honest, I'm a bit behind on… well, everything. Shopping, decorating – I haven't had much time to get it all done. Are you ready for the holidays?"

"Sure am!" he exclaimed, excitement bubbling over in his voice. "Got my tree up, presents wrapped, and I'll be heading out of town to see the family soon."

"Oh, wow. You're really prepared," she said, not hiding any of her insecurity.

"Aw, don't worry yourself too much, April. You've already accomplished so much this year." Chuck patted her shoulder reassuringly. "Besides, you did a miracle on that house."

"Thank you. You're right," she agreed, her lips curving into a small smile. But deep down, she couldn't shake the creeping frustration that everyone seemed to be asking her about Christmas when she was already struggling to juggle her daily responsibilities.

She wasn't ready for Christmas. At least not as well as she had been in the past. Her mother used to create such wonderful Christmas parties.

"Anyway, I should get going. Lots of shopping to do," April said with a forced laugh, eager to change the topic. "It was nice seeing you, Chuck."

"Same to you, April. And don't forget: take some time for yourself this season. You deserve it." Chuck waved as April walked deeper into the store, her determination to find the perfect gifts for her friends and family fueling her every step.

Take some time for yourself, she pondered, repeating his words in her mind.

It was a nice sentiment, but she knew that wouldn't ease the stress of trying to make everything perfect for those she cared about. As she browsed through the various aisles, the weight of her task seemed to grow heavier, but she was resolute in her mission to make this holiday season one to remember.

April pushed her cart, the wheels squeaking softly as she navigated the maze of aisles. Her eyes darted from shelf to shelf, scanning for a gift that would not only be something Georgia could use but also convey her love and appreciation.

The store's twinkling lights shone brightly over the tall racks, creating an almost magical atmosphere. Still, deep down, April felt the ticking clock as everyone else seemed to be prepared for the magic of the holiday.

The heated blanket she first thought of caught her eye – its plush fabric beckoning her. She knew it would work. Georgia would certainly use it.

After pushing the soft fabric between her fingers, she tossed it in the cart. But she knew she also had to find something more personal, something that spoke to their unique bond.

As April continued her search, she wandered into an aisle filled with an assortment of knickknacks. The shelves were lined with figurines and collectible glassware.

April sighed, frustration etching her face as she scanned the trinkets one last time. Her eyes fell on a porcelain cat, a wooden sailboat, and a glass dolphin, but none seemed to hold the personal touch she was searching for.

She straightened her back and glanced around, catching sight of the jewelry section just a few steps away.

April didn't have high hopes for the section, but at least she could browse the gorgeous silver pieces.

As she meandered through the rows of necklaces, bracelets, and rings, a small elephant pendant caught her eye. A smile spread across her face as she recalled Kristy's story about her childhood love for elephants and how they symbolized home.

Kristy would love something so adorable. And she knew she wanted to get her something from the bed and breakfast for all of her help. She picked up the delicate necklace and admiring its intricate details. She placed it gently in her cart, feeling a sense of accomplishment at having found a heartfelt gift.

"Alright, Georgia," she whispered, scanning the jewelry section with renewed determination. "Your turn."

Her gaze settled on a small wooden jewelry box nestled among other trinkets. The letter 'G' was elegantly engraved on its top, and the sight of it sent a wave of nostalgia washing over her; it looked strikingly similar to a box she had received when she was young, filled with childhood memories and treasures.

April wondered if her daughter would cherish something similar. She imagined her daughter's green eyes lighting up as they shared stories of their past and dreams for the future. The simple yet elegant design, coupled with the sentimental significance, made it the perfect gift for her beloved daughter.

With a satisfied sigh, April added the jewelry box to her cart, her heart swelling with the anticipation of giving these thoughtful gifts to those she held dear. She took a moment to appreciate her finds before pushing her cart towards the checkout, the wheels squeaking softly in approval.

April wondered if she really was so unprepared after all. She's checked off a few boxes, but there were still plenty left.

Despite being pressed for time and the stresses that accompanied the holiday season, April had found a way to show her love and appreciation for those who meant the most to her.

Knowing she needed to get back to the ranch soon, April headed towards the checkout. Near the checkout counters was a display of pocket knives. One in particular had a gorgeous stallion carved into the blade.

It would have been perfect for Jackson. Which made April question if she was supposed to get him a gift.

As the doubt gnawed at her, April picked up the pocket knife, turning it over in her hands. She couldn't deny the thoughtfulness of the gift, and yet she couldn't shake the lingering uncertainty.

If he was here with her, she would have gotten him a gift without a second thought. But now, she wasn't even sure he'd be around for her to give him a gift. She wasn't sure if she would ever see him again.

CHAPTER FOUR

The chilly December air nipped at April's cheeks as she hurried into the bed and breakfast, arms laden with shopping bags. The scent of cinnamon and pine filled her nostrils while the warmth of the B&B embraced her like a long-lost friend.

"Mom, there you are!" Georgia called out from across the room, her green eyes sparkling with curiosity. "What do you have there?"

"Nothing," April stammered, quickly hiding the bags behind her back. Her heart raced as she recalled the unique and carefully chosen gifts nestled within the colorful paper. She couldn't let Georgia see them just yet; they were meant for Christmas morning.

"Really?" Georgia raised an eyebrow, a playful smirk dancing on her lips. "Well, I brought back that coffee you wanted." She held up a small brown cup, the tantalizing aroma of locally made coffee wafting through the air.

"Thank you, sweetheart," April said, gratefully accepting the offering. She inhaled deeply, savoring the rich scent. For a moment, the weight of the world seemed to lift off her shoulders – but only for a moment.

"Anyway," Georgia continued, her attention returning to the shopping bags concealed behind her mother. "I've got to head out and do some Christmas shopping of my own. You know how it is."

"Of course," April replied, her smile genuine but tinged with disappointment. Though she wanted to keep Christmas a surprise, she wished that her daughter would stick around the house more during her time off from school. "Have fun, and be careful out there."

"Will do," Georgia assured her before wrapping her arms around April in a warm embrace. "Love you, Mom."

"Love you too, honey." April squeezed her tight, cherishing the simple joy of their connection. After a moment, they pulled apart, and Georgia waved goodbye before disappearing out the door.

Alone at last, April let out a quiet sigh, her thoughts turning to the gifts and the anticipation of sharing them with her loved ones.

She felt a twinge of sadness as she thought of one person in particular – someone who might never know just how much he meant to her. She regretted not getting that gift for Jackson at the store.

But maybe it wasn't too late. There had to be something she could do to stop thinking about him. Something to figure out what happened that he had to leave in such a hurry.

In the dim light of her room, April carefully stowed the shopping bags behind her dresser, ensuring that their contents remained safely hidden from prying eyes.

Her heart swelled with warmth as she imagined the delighted reactions those presents would evoke on Christmas morning. However, duty called, and the ranch wouldn't run itself.

She still had to check on the horses, ensuring they didn't need any gauze changes.

She slipped out of the room and made her way back to the bustling lobby.

The aroma of freshly brewed coffee greeted her as she entered, mingling with the scents of pine and cinnamon that lingered in the air. The walls felt bare without any holiday decorations, but that was why she grabbed some at the store while she was gift shopping.

"Welcome in," Kristy, the ever-cheerful receptionist, chirped from behind the front desk.

A newlywed couple stood before her, their hands entwined and expressions brimming with affection. April couldn't help but watch them from a distance; their love was almost palpable, and it stirred something deep within her.

"Thank you," the woman replied, her voice soft and melodic. "We're so excited to spend our first Christmas together."

"Sounds lovely," Kristy said, her fingers dancing over the computer keyboard as she entered their reservation details. "What brings you to our quaint little town?"

"We thought it would be nice to have some time away before joining our families for the holidays," the man answered, giving his wife a tender smile that made April's heart ache with longing.

"Perfect," Kristy enthused, handing them their room key with a warm grin. "Well, we're very glad you chose to stay with us. I'll give you these, and then I can check you in here."

As April watched them, she felt a pang of envy. She longed for that kind of connection – to have someone who looked at her with such love and devotion. But her thoughts inevitably drifted toward Jackson.

She guessed that it was fate trying to punish her for some reason. At every turn, she seemed to find something to remind her of him. She was trying to run from it, but the whole world seemed to be deciding she needed to face it head-on.

As the newlywed couple continued their conversation with Kristy, April observed them more closely. The man held his wife gently around her shoulders, fingers resting lightly on her arm, as if she were a treasure too delicate to hold tightly.

She leaned into him, her head resting against his chest in quiet contentment, a soft smile gracing her lips. Their shared warmth created a bubble of love around them, and it was impossible not to be drawn in.

"Did you see that little bookstore down the street?" the woman asked her husband, her eyes lighting up with excitement. "I thought maybe we could pick up some novels to read together by the fire tonight."

"Sounds perfect," he agreed, his voice warm and tender. "And perhaps later, we can take a walk under the stars."

"Only if I get to wear your coat," she teased, her fingers playing with the lapel of his jacket. He chuckled softly, pressing a kiss to her forehead.

"Anything for you, my love."

April felt an ache in her chest, watching the easy affection between them. As they made their way up the stairs, laughter trailing behind them, Kristy turned to April with a knowing smile.

"They're absolutely adorable, aren't they?" she said, leaning her elbows on the counter. "You can just feel how much they love each other."

April nodded, her thoughts still lingering on Jackson. "I hope to get that someday," she admitted quietly, her fingers fiddling with the edge of the receptionist's desk. "Someone who would look at me like that."

Kristy's gaze softened. "Well, Georgia mentioned that ranch hand you've been getting close to," she ventured, her tone light but probing. "The way you two looked at each other...it seemed like there might be something there."

"Maybe," April sighed, her heart heavy with uncertainty. "But he's gone now, and I don't know if we'll ever get the chance to find out."

"April," Kristy said gently, placing a reassuring hand on her arm, "sometimes, all it takes is a little courage to find what you're looking for."

"Jackson and I are just friends," April replied, her eyes unable to focus on any one thing as she thought of him. "At least, that's what we were before he left... I just can't believe he left that short note and nothing else. I want to know what happened, but I don't want to bother him."

Kristy studied her for a moment, understanding shining in her eyes. "You know, April, if you want to tell him how you feel, there's a way to do that."

Seeing the curiosity in April's gaze, she continued, "You're his boss, right? And you have his contact information for emergencies. Technically, you'd just be checking up on an employee if you went to see if he was there."

April bit her lip, her mind racing with this new possibility. Was it really okay to just show up at Jackson's house and ask to see him? It might work in romance movies, but was it okay to do in real life? She worried about him, that much was true, but would it be going too far to invade his privacy like this?

"Maybe," she murmured, still hesitating. "But what if he doesn't want to see me? What if he isn't even there?" The vulnerability in her voice betrayed her deeper fears, and Kristy reached out to squeeze her hand reassuringly.

"April, you'll never know if you don't try," Kristy said gently. "And if it turns out he needs someone right now, wouldn't you rather be there for him?"

As her new worker's words sank in, April took a deep breath, feeling a mix of anticipation and anxiety coursing through her veins. "You're right," she admitted, determination slowly creeping into her voice. "I won't know unless I try."

Kristy pulled out a small white binder from behind the desk and set it in front of April. It held all of the employees information in case of emergencies. April had showed it to her on her first day of work. And now, she was clearly prompting April to use it herself.

"Okay, I'll think about it," April finally conceded, her voice wavering with uncertainty. She reached out to take the employee binder from Kristy, her fingers brushing against her's reassuringly.

"Good luck, April," Kristy said with a supportive smile. "I truly hope everything works out for you."

"Thanks, Kristy," April replied softly, giving her a grateful nod before retreating to her room.

As she closed the door behind her, April found herself surrounded by the few festive decorations and items she had purchased at the store. The twinkling fairy lights and soft reds and greens of the ornaments seemed to mock her current emotional turmoil.

She picked up a delicate ornament, shaped like a heart, and stared at it for a moment. If only mending her own heart could be as simple as hanging it on a tree.

Shaking her head, she realized she was unable to focus on the task at hand. With great care, she opened the binder to Jackson's paperwork, seeking out his address. There it was, scribbled in Jackson's distinct handwriting - a lifeline to the man who had slipped away from her so suddenly.

"Here goes nothing," she whispered to herself, feeling an odd mixture of excitement and trepidation. Her heart raced as she grabbed her coat and keys, heading towards her car.

She waved to Kristy on her way out, who gave her a knowing glance. "I'll be back in about two hours," she called out as she left.

The crisp winter air nipped at April's cheeks as she stepped outside, a tangible reminder of the importance of connection and warmth during the holiday season. She climbed into her car and, with shaking hands, input the address into her GPS.

She sighed as the device calculated her route. This was it. It was time to make sure Jackson was okay. And maybe time to tell him that she felt something for him. April wasn't sure how it would all turn out.

But this felt like the right thing to do.

With newfound resolve, April put the car in gear and began driving towards the barn. She stepped out in a hurry and looked in each stall, ensuring that their wounds were still wrapped tightly and not bled through.

When she knew it was safe, she climbed back into her car and began to take off down the driveway.

As the familiar landscape of her small ranch began to fade in the distance, her thoughts were consumed by the image of Jackson's kind eyes and gentle touch.

"Please let this be the right thing to do," she prayed silently, feeling a strange sense of calm wash over her as she continued on her journey.

For better or worse, she knew that she had to see this through – not just for herself, but for the possibility of a future with Jackson that seemed to grow ever more precious with each passing moment.

She was determined to make sure Jackson was okay.

***

April's knuckles turned white as she gripped the steering wheel tightly, her heart racing with a mixture of anxiety and determination. A stray lock of her dark hair fell across her forehead, but she didn't bother to brush it away. Instead, her gaze remained fixed on the winding road ahead.

Was she completely out of her mind? Her breath caught as she wondered what she was doing driving to a stranger's house in the middle of the day.

An hour ago, she had been filled with a sense of purpose, an unwavering conviction that she needed to find Jackson. But now, as the miles ticked by, doubt began to creep in like an invasive weed.

Was she really doing this? Was she truly driving miles and miles to hunt down her ranch hand just because she didn't know what happened? He meant a lot to her, of course, but was she about to bother him as he was trying to get away from her?

As she approached the quiet town nestled amongst rolling hills, her GPS chirped cheerily, indicating that she was getting close. The picturesque scene before her seemed at odds with the whirlwind of emotions inside her.

She glanced around at the quaint houses, the well-manicured lawns, and the friendly faces of people walking the roads, faces she didn't know. What would they think if they knew what she was doing? More importantly, what would Jackson think?

Was it too late to turn back now? What if he thought of her differently? Like she was some kind of stalker?

Then she thought about it. Technically, she was tracking him down, but only to make sure he was okay. Only to ask if she'd done something to push him away.

She pulled over for a moment, taking a deep breath and trying to silence the doubts that threatened to drown out her original resolve. This wasn't about her pride or how she might appear to others, she reminded herself. This was about more than that, about understanding the sudden distance that had formed between them.

She told herself to get it together as she gripped the steering wheel firmly. She needed to know what had happened – not just for herself, but for the friendship they had built. And if that meant driving into the unknown and taking a risk, so be it.

"Here goes nothing," she murmured, pressing her foot down on the gas pedal and continuing onward toward her destination – and whatever awaited her there.

The sun dipped low on the horizon, casting a warm glow on the quiet town that lay nestled in the rolling hills. April's eyes scanned the landscape as her mind raced with questions she couldn't suppress any longer.

She recalled the vague note Jackson had left her, which only served to deepen her confusion. A simple call or text would have been enough to answer her lingering queries – but that never came. Now, here she was, chasing after him like some lost soul searching for answers.

"Ugh, this is so frustrating," she sighed, tapping her fingers rhythmically on the wheel.

As her car hummed along the winding road, April found herself reminiscing about their conversations – the way they'd bonded. They had forged a connection that felt genuine, and Jackson had always seemed eager to be her friend.

April had to convince herself again of all of the fun times they'd had together. The times working on the ranch and preparing for the horses. The time he came to the town hall meeting to support her and the fight for the native animals.

Clearly, she meant something to him. There was no doubt that they were friends, at the very least. And didn't that warrant something? Didn't that mean something to him?

In that moment, her determination resurfaced, and she knew she couldn't turn back now. She needed to see Jackson to ask him directly about his sudden disappearance from her life.

April steeled herself for the confrontation she was about to face.

The sun cast a warm golden hue over the quaint town, painting the rolling hills with an ethereal glow. April's heart pounded in her chest, her palms slightly clammy against the steering wheel.

She had come this far, driven all this way to find Jackson and get her answers. There was no turning back now.

"Okay, deep breaths, April," she whispered to herself, steadying her nerves as she pulled up to a nice house in the middle of a large plot of land. The field was deep and full of pastures filled with beloved animals.

The farmhouse was a charming sight, with its vibrant blue shutters and flower boxes overflowing with colorful blooms. The wraparound porch was adorned with a delicate wooden railing.

In the distance, April could hear the babbling of a creek that hid behind the house. She could almost taste the sweetness of the wildflowers in the air. And the soft rustling of the wind in the surrounding trees set her heart at ease.

The scent of lavender from a nearby garden filled the air, adding a sense of tranquility to the moment that belied the turmoil raging within her.

As she stepped out of her car, a gentle breeze rustled through the leaves overhead, setting off a symphony of birdsong. It felt like nature itself was urging her on, lending her the courage to confront Jackson about his sudden departure from her life.

When she finally gained the courage, she approached the front door and held up a hand to knock. She hesitated.

What she was about to do could change her relationship with her friend forever. Her hand shook as she rapped it against the door. And she stepped back and waited for him to answer.

CHAPTER FIVE

Worry gnawed at the edges of April's thoughts as she stood on the unfamiliar doorstep, her heart pounding in her chest. The cozy, unassuming house had a well-tended garden with colorful flowers that seemed to mock her anxiety. With a trembling hand, she knocked on the door and held her breath.

She heard footsteps growing louder until they reached the other side of the door. As it creaked open, a little boy appeared before her. His wide, inquisitive eyes met hers, and his brow furrowed in confusion.

A cold terror gripped April as she stared back at him, her mind racing. Was this Jackson's child? Did he have a family he had never mentioned?

Was she in love with someone who already had a family? Did she embarrass herself weeks ago when she had to tell him that they should stay friends?

"Who are you?" the boy asked, his voice filled with curiosity.

April hesitated, her mouth feeling dry. "I… I'm sorry. I think I'm at the wrong house." She forced a smile, attempting to hide her panic. Her heart was a wild bird inside her chest, desperate to escape its cage.

"Okay," the boy replied uncertainly, still clinging to the doorframe.

She turned to leave, utterly embarrassed and ready to never return.

"April?"

Her ears recognized the familiar timbre of Jackson's voice from behind her. Not only did he sound happy to see her – there was warmth in his tone that she wasn't expecting in the slightest.

"April!" Jackson called out, stepping into view. His light eyes sparkled with genuine surprise and delight, and his short, messy hair gleamed under the afternoon sun. "What are you doing here?"

"Jackson…" she breathed, relief washing over her like a wave. "I just… I needed to see you."

"Is everything okay?" His gentle concern melted her heart even further. And as they stood there, the world around them faded away, leaving only the two of them standing on the precipice of something new and unknown.

"Actually, I found your address on your emergency contact form," April admitted sheepishly, her cheeks flushing with embarrassment. "You left so suddenly, and I was worried about you. I just wanted to make sure you were okay."

Jackson's eyes softened at her confession, a gentle smile playing on his lips. "I appreciate your concern, April. I'm sorry if I caused you any worry."

The words tumbled out before she could stop them, emotions rising like a tide within her. "I need you to come back, Jackson. I miss you."

Her heart thumped loudly in her ears as she continued, "I like really miss you. It's been so hard to get everything done around the ranch. There's like a thousand things to do, and it was so much easier when you were there. And maybe I feel something for you."

For a moment, there was silence between them; the air seemed to vibrate with unspoken tension. The little boy had long since retreated into the house, leaving the two adults to face each other on the porch.

As they stood there, the world around them seemingly suspended in time, April became acutely aware of the rustling leaves in the breeze, the distant chirping of birds, and the warmth of the sun on her skin. She glanced down at her hands, fidgeting nervously with the hem of her shirt, waiting for Jackson's response.

Finally, Jackson opened his mouth to say something, but hesitated. His light eyes searched her face, as if trying to read her thoughts.

She could feel her heart pounding in her chest as she stood before Jackson, his light eyes fixed on her with an intensity that made her shiver.

"Say something," she whispered, unable to bear the weight of his silence any longer. Her mind raced, trying to recall every detail of their previous conversations, searching for some clue as to what he might be thinking.

When he had first arrived at her property, she had found him reserved and enigmatic, but over time, she had seen glimpses of the kind, passionate man underneath. And now, she desperately longed for him to open up once more.

She used to love that he was mysterious, but now she couldn't handle his long, poignant pauses. His looks that never divulged his true feelings. She couldn't read him, and it drove her crazy.

Jackson's gaze never wavered, and she felt as if he could see straight into her soul, reading her every thought and desire. She bit her lip involuntarily, her breath catching in her throat as she waited for him to speak.

And then he smiled – a gentle, genuine smile that made her heart swell with warmth and affection. "April," he began, his voice low and tender, "I'm glad you came."

"Really?" she asked tentatively, hope blossoming within her. "Because ever since you left the other day, I've been going crazy trying to figure out what happened."

He looked away for a moment, his eyes drifting toward the darkening sky before returning to meet hers. "To be honest," he said quietly, "I'm not so sure I care about any of that right now. Did I hear you right? You want to be with me?"

Her breath caught in her throat before she responded, "Yes. That is what I said."

Jackson looked her up and down. "I'd like that."

Her heart skipped a beat at his words, the last remnants of doubt evaporating as she drank in the sincerity etched across his handsome features. The former lawyer in her wanted to cross-examine him, to ask a dozen more questions and dissect every nuance of their relationship.

But for once, she chose to silence that part of herself and simply revel in the joy of knowing they both wanted the same thing.

"Actually?" she murmured, her voice barely audible above the gentle rustling of the leaves around them.

"Of course," he replied, his smile deepening. "We have this connection between us. I can't deny that."

April nodded, unable to conceal her own smile any longer as she looked into Jackson's eyes – no longer a mystery, but a window into a future she never knew she wanted until now.

The sun dipped below the horizon, casting a golden glow on their faces as Jackson took a tentative step forward. April's heart raced, her pulse quickening with each inch he closed between them.

The air around them was thick with anticipation, charged with an energy that made the hairs on the back of her neck stand on end.

"April," Jackson whispered, his voice like a warm caress, sending shivers down her spine. She looked into his eyes, the light within them reflecting the last remnants of the day as it faded into twilight. "Can I...?"

She nodded, barely able to form the words with how tightly her throat constricted with emotion. "Yes, please."

He moved closer, bridging the gap between them until she could feel the heat emanating from his body. She noticed the fine lines that framed his eyes when he smiled and the way he swallowed nervously. As he leaned in, she caught a whiff of his scent – a mixture of earth and sweat, with a hint of something uniquely his own.

Their lips brushed together tentatively at first, a whisper of a touch. April's fingers found their way to the nape of his neck, gently urging him closer, and Jackson responded in kind, deepening the kiss as his hands came to rest on her hips.

In that moment, all thoughts of her past, her divorce, and her life before the small town seemed to vanish, replaced by the warmth of Jackson's embrace and the tender passion of his touch. Her doubts and fears were washed away as they shared their first kiss beneath the canopy of the rustling trees.

As they finally broke apart, April's mind raced with a tumult of emotions. Excitement, happiness, and a sense of belonging she hadn't felt in years all swirled together, leaving her lightheaded and eager for more.

"Wow," was all she managed to say, her voice shaky with the intensity of what they had just experienced together.

"Indeed," Jackson murmured, his thumb gently caressing her cheek. "I've been wanting to do that for a long time."

"Me too," April admitted, a blush creeping onto her cheeks. "What do you think this means for us?"

He smiled, his gaze never leaving hers. "I think it means we're embarking on something wonderful, April. And I can't wait to see where it takes us."

CHAPTER SIX

April perched gracefully on a wooden stool in the charming farmhouse kitchen, her dark hair framing her face as she took in the warm atmosphere of the room. The sunlight streamed in through the window, casting an inviting glow on the rustic countertops and vintage decor. She ran her fingers over the smooth surface of the worn table that had clearly been the center of many family meals.

"Here you go," Jackson said softly, setting two steaming mugs of tea down on the table. His light eyes sparkled as he pulled up a stool next to April. "I hope chamomile is alright."

"Perfect, thank you," April replied, wrapping her hands around the mug, feeling the warmth seep into her fingertips.

She hesitated for a moment before gathering the courage to ask the question that had been nagging at her since she arrived. "Jackson, if I may... Why did you leave? I was really worried about you."

Jackson's eyes fell to his own mug, cradling it in his strong, calloused hands. He sighed, the weight of his unspoken thoughts seeming to rest heavily on his broad shoulders.

"My sister got sick," he explained, his voice barely above a whisper. "She needed surgery and I couldn't let her go through it alone. So, I came here to help with the kids and the house."

A mixture of relief and sympathy washed over April as she listened to Jackson's words. It hadn't been anything she had done or said that had caused him to leave so abruptly. Her heart ached for him and his family, knowing how much they must be going through.

April's heart swelled with empathy, and she couldn't help but feel a pang of guilt for having intruded during such a difficult time. The steam from the tea rose between them, creating a momentary veil that softened their expressions.

"Jackson, I had no idea," April said earnestly, her dark eyes filled with concern. "I'm so sorry for barging in like this. If I'd known, I wouldn't have... I was just really worried about you." She hesitated, her voice barely more than a whisper.

He looked up and offered her a small smile, his eyes reflecting a quiet gratitude for her understanding. "Thanks, April. It's just... family comes first, you know?"

"Of course," April agreed, her thoughts drifting back to her own life and the choices she had made in pursuit of happiness.

Moving to the small town, leaving behind a successful legal career, and renovating her childhood home into a bed and breakfast had all been driven by her desire for connection and community.

"If I'd known, I would have never come. I just didn't know if I'd done something wrong or if you were hurt somewhere."

Jackson shook his head, his light eyes meeting hers with a reassuring warmth. "No, April, it's not your fault at all. I should be the one apologizing." He took a sip of his tea before continuing. "I tried to convey that I would be back, but clearly I'm not very good with my words." He offered her a half-smile, an expression that spoke of both regret and gratitude for her presence. "I just wasn't sure how much time I would need."

He set down his teacup, his gaze steady on hers. "And I saw that you called. I was planning on calling you back when we heard that the surgery went well, but my nephew – the little cutie who answered the door for you – well, he dropped my phone into the toilet." Jackson chuckled softly, the sound easing the tension that had settled over them.

She marveled at how, even in the midst of hardship, he managed to find a way to smile. It was a quality she admired and longed to emulate. With every word he spoke, she found herself falling deeper under his spell, entranced by his kindness and resilience.

As they sat together in the cozy kitchen, sipping their tea and sharing a moment of quiet understanding, April realized that while their paths may have been different, she and Jackson both valued the importance of love and support.

It was yet another reason why she found herself drawn to him, and she wondered what the future might hold for them as they navigated their lives in this quaint little town.

"Kids will be kids," April replied with a small laugh, her cheeks warming as she envisioned the mischievous grin of Jackson's nephew. "I'm just glad everything is okay now." She wrapped her hands around her teacup, drawing comfort from its warmth and the soothing scent of the tea.

"Thank you, April," Jackson murmured, his eyes reflecting a quiet appreciation that warmed her soul. "Your concern means more to me than you know. I can't tell you how nice it is to see a friendly face."

As they sat there in the cozy kitchen, sharing their thoughts and fears, April felt a sense of belonging she hadn't experienced in years. No matter what challenges life threw at them, she knew deep down that together, they could face anything.

A soft breeze rustled the lace curtains in the charming farmhouse kitchen, casting a warm glow over the room. April admired the intricate details of the quaint space – the delicate floral wallpaper, the vintage teapot that whistled gently on the stove, and the worn wooden stool that supported her as she sat beside Jackson.

"Jackson," April began, her voice faltering ever so slightly, "I feel so silly for having panicked like I did." She shook her head, hair framing her face as she bit her lip in self-reproach. "I have this terrible habit of overthinking everything, and sometimes it gets me into trouble."

She glanced at him, her fingers nervously tracing the rim of her teacup. "I should have waited until you returned instead of barging into your life like this," she admitted, her cheeks flushing a deep shade of pink.

Inside, she was eating herself alive with regret. Though it was incredibly difficult for her to sit and wait for weeks before hearing anything, she should have trusted that if something was wrong, she would hear about it.

More information would have been nice, but it wasn't his job to keep her updated about everything. He left a note, which should have been enough for her to trust him.

Something told April to go after him. And it built and built until she couldn't take it anymore, and she needed to see him by any means necessary. Now, of course, she wished she hadn't acted on it.

"April," Jackson replied gently, his light eyes full of warmth and understanding, "there is no need for you to apologize." He reached across the small space between them, placing his large, calloused hand over hers, offering comfort and reassurance. "In fact, I'm glad you're here with me now."

He paused, letting his gaze drift towards the window, as if searching for the right words among the swaying branches outside. "I should have been more clear in my note," he confessed, his voice tinged with regret. "I left things vague because I wasn't sure how long

I'd be gone or how the surgery would go. But please, don't blame yourself for worrying."

As he spoke, a bittersweet smile played upon his lips, revealing the depth of his kindness and concern. April marveled at the quiet strength that seemed to emanate from him, even as he bore the weight of his sister's illness and the uncertainty of the situation.

For a moment, they simply sat there, hands entwined, allowing the gentle hum of the kitchen to envelop them in its soothing embrace. In the midst of their shared vulnerability and understanding, something profound unfurled between them – a connection that transcended words, a recognition of kindred spirits finding solace in one another.

"Thank you, Jackson," April murmured, her heart swelling with gratitude and affection for this man who had so quickly become an integral part of her life.

"Anytime, April," he replied softly, his eyes meeting hers with a promise of unwavering support. "You're not alone anymore."

Just as the last remnants of tension seemed to dissipate, the kitchen door swung open with a gentle creak. A woman with a warm smile and eyes that mirrored Jackson's stepped in, her gaze falling on the two of them.

"Jackson," she began before turning her attention to April. "You must be April! It's so nice to finally meet you." She extended a hand, which April took, noting the strength hidden beneath her delicate appearance.

"April, this is my sister Julia," Jackson said, pride evident in his voice. "Julia, I thought you were supposed to be napping."

"Oh, please. I'm going to in a bit. I can take care of myself now, remember?" she replied, rolling her eyes playfully. "I'm doing just fine now, but I could use some help finding my medication."

"Of course, let me—" Jackson began, but Julia waved him off with a laugh.

"Relax, Jackson. I can manage. You should show April around the property. I've heard so much about you," she said, turning to April. "It's about time she sees the place for herself," she insisted with a knowing smile.

Jackson glanced at April, who felt a sudden flush creeping up her cheeks. "I don't want to impose," she stammered, unsure how to navigate this unexpected development.

"Please, it's no trouble," Julia assured her. "Besides, I need to put my son down for a nap soon. He's been quite the handful today."

"Are you sure?" Jackson asked, torn between his concern for his sister and his desire to spend more time with April.

"Positive," Julia replied firmly, steering them both towards the door. "Now go on, before I change my mind."

With a final glance back at his sister, Jackson reluctantly agreed. As he led April out into the sunlit yard, the warmth of the day seemed to wrap itself around her like a comforting embrace. She couldn't help but feel that despite the rocky start, this visit had turned into an opportunity to deepen her connection with Jackson.

CHAPTER SEVEN

The sun dipped below the horizon, casting a warm golden glow on the lush, green pasture. The gentle babbling of the creek in the distance created a serene melody that harmonized with the soft whinnies of the horses and the contented clucks of the chickens that roamed the grass.

Along the fence line, the oaks and willows reached toward the sky, their branches swaying gently in the breeze. April let out a sigh of pure contentment as she leaned against the wooden fence, Jackson by her side.

"See that one over there?" Jackson pointed to a chestnut mare with a white blaze running down her face. "That's Bailey. And next to her is May, our resident troublemaker."

April smiled as she watched the horses interact, feeling a connection to these beautiful creatures that seemed to embody the spirit of this tranquil place. She turned her attention back to Jackson, his light eyes shimmering with warmth and kindness.

"Jackson, I have to say, this ranch is truly breathtaking," she said, her voice filled with genuine admiration.

"Thank you, April. It's been a labor of love for me," he replied, a hint of pride in his voice.

As the gentle breeze tousled his short, messy hair, Jackson looked at her intently. His eyes seemed to be searching for something, perhaps the courage to share what was on his mind. April could sense there was more to him than met the eye – a depth that intrigued her.

"April, there's something I've been wanting to tell you about my feelings for a while now," Jackson began hesitantly. "Because you were with Nigel, I didn't think it would be right. And I knew how much stress you've been under lately, dealing with your divorce and renovating the bed and breakfast. I wanted to help, but I thought it was best to keep my distance."

April felt her heart swell with affection as she realized the extent of Jackson's consideration for her feelings. She had always been drawn to his kindness, but this only served to deepen her appreciation for him.

"Jackson, that's so sweet of you," she said softly, her dark eyes meeting his.

She hadn't realized he had been so thoughtful all along. She couldn't have asked for anyone more considerate. He was the kindest she had found yet.

They stood there for a moment, exchanging a tender gaze as the sun continued to set, casting a warm glow over the beautiful ranch and the two people who now found themselves drawn even closer together in the light of honesty and understanding.

Taking a deep breath, April decided it was time to share more of her own feelings with Jackson. It was about time they were able to be candid with one another.

As they stood there, the soft nicker of horses and gentle rustling of leaves in the background, she gathered her thoughts, feeling both vulnerable and excited.

"Jackson, I have to admit something too," April began, her voice wavering slightly. "I've always been interested in you. But I was terrified to try it out. Things with Nigel weren't working, and I couldn't help but wonder 'what if' about us. I didn't know what to do about it."

She looked down at her hands, twisting them nervously in front of her. "I felt like it wasn't fair to Nigel when there was clearly something between you and me. And that's part of the reason we've left each other, I want to see where this might lead."

At her words, Jackson's eyes lit up, and a simple, mysterious smile tugged at the corners of his mouth. It was the kind of smile that had always pulled her in – one that hinted at a world of hidden depths beneath his quiet exterior. He didn't say anything right away, which only served to mystify April further.

"Jackson?" she asked, curious. "What's going on in your head?"

In response, he reached out slowly, brushing a stray strand of hair away from her face with a tender touch. The warmth of his fingers sent a shiver down her spine, and she found herself holding her breath, waiting for his answer.

"April," he finally said, his voice low and warm. "I'm just happy to be here with you right now, in this beautiful place. And I'm so glad you came."

As he spoke, their eyes locked once more, and April could feel the connection between them growing stronger by the second. In that moment, the future seemed full of possibilities, and she couldn't wait to see what lay ahead for them both.

April giggled, her happiness bubbling up and spilling over like the water in the nearby creek. She looked into Jackson's eyes, full of warmth and sincerity, and felt a sense of peace that had been missing for far too long.

"I'm really happy, too," she admitted, her heart swelling with emotion. "So, what's next for us?" She glanced around at the ranch, taking in the animals and the beauty of their surroundings. "I mean, I'll obviously be leaving to go home soon, and you need to stay here and take care of Julia until she feels better."

Jackson leaned against the fence, his strong arms crossed over his chest as he contemplated her question. The sun cast a halo around his dark hair, making him look almost ethereal. April could see the wheels turning in his head as he weighed his options.

"Actually," he said after a moment, the corner of his mouth quirking up into a half-smile. "I was planning on coming back to town in the next week or so. I want to be there for Christmas, and Julia needs some time on her own to regain her strength without me hovering over her." He paused, looking thoughtful, before continuing. "So, I guess we just... begin dating?"

April felt her heart skip a beat at the thought, excitement and anticipation coursing through her veins. This was new territory for both of them, but it felt so right. She nodded, a wide grin spreading across her face.

"That sounds great," she agreed, taking a step closer to him. The air between them seemed to crackle with electricity, and she couldn't help but reach out to touch his arm, feeling the reassuring solidity of him beneath her fingers.

As they stood together, surrounded by the beauty of the ranch and the gentle babble of the creek, April found herself brimming with hope. This was a fresh start for both of them, a chance to explore their feelings and see where life would take them.

And as she looked into Jackson's eyes, full of warmth and promise, she knew that whatever the future held, they were ready to face it together.

CHAPTER EIGHT

A week had flown by like an autumn leaf caught in the wind, and April found herself humming a festive tune as she draped garland around the banister of the lobby staircase. The bed and breakfast was slowly transforming into a cozy haven for the holidays – twinkling fairy lights adorned the windows, and the scent of cinnamon and cloves filled the air. She caught her reflection in one of the shiny ornaments - her dark hair tied back in a loose ponytail, a rosy blush on her cheeks from all the exertion.

"April, do you need any help with that?" Kristy's cheerful voice cut through her reverie.

"Thanks, but I've got it," April replied with a smile, looping the last piece of garland into place. "It's starting to feel more festive in here, don't you think?"

Kristy nodded, her eyes gleaming with excitement. "It's lovely. You're doing a fantastic job."

"Thank you." April paused for a moment, glancing at the antique grandfather clock near the entrance. "I'm trying to get the place ready because Jackson should be back in town today. I can hardly wait to see him again."

"Really? That's wonderful!" Kristy exclaimed, her gaze softening as she observed the warmth in April's expression. "I'm so glad you decided to go after your feelings, April. You deserve happiness, and if Jackson is what your heart desires, then you should absolutely pursue it."

April blushed at Kristy's words, her chest swelling with gratitude. It felt incredible to have someone in her corner, cheering her on. "Thank you, Kristy. That means a lot to me." She sighed, her thoughts drifting to Jackson – his kind, light eyes, and his gentle, mysterious demeanor. "It felt good to let everything out."

"Congratulations. What a beautiful thing," Kristy responded, giving her a knowing smile. "Now, let's finish up with these decorations so you can greet him with the perfect holiday atmosphere!"

"Agreed!" April said enthusiastically, feeling a renewed sense of purpose. She couldn't wait to see Jackson again, and she was determined to make the bed and breakfast as inviting and festive as possible for his return. With Kristy by her side, she knew they'd create the perfect setting for love to blossom.

April watched as Kristy expertly arranged a cluster of holly and ivy on the mantle, marveling at how easily she had adapted to life at the bed and breakfast. It seemed like a stroke of fate that Kristy had come into her life just when she needed help the most, especially with the holiday season upon them.

"Kristy, I don't know what I would do without you," April admitted, a genuine grin spreading across her face. "You're an absolute lifesaver."

"Aw, shucks, April. I'm just happy to be here," Kristy replied, returning the smile warmly. "I love this place, and I can see how much it means to you."

As they continued decorating, April couldn't shake the nagging feeling that time was running out. She wanted everything to be perfect for Jackson's return – not just festive, but romantic as well. Her heart raced in anticipation, and she found herself glancing at the door more often than she'd care to admit.

It wasn't just Jackson that she was trying to impress either. Somewhere deep down, she wanted Georgia to see the Christmas spirit in this place and get excited for the holiday. Maybe later, she could talk her into helping them decorate.

"Okay, how about we hang some mistletoe?" Kristy suggested. "It'll add a nice touch of romance to the place."

"Great idea!" April agreed, her eyes lighting up. "Let's put some over the entrance and maybe a couple more in strategic locations around the lobby."

As they moved to carry out their plan, footsteps echoed through the lobby, drawing their attention. A guest, wrapped in a thick sweater and scarf, appeared at the top of the stairs and called down to Kristy, her breath visible in the chilly air.

"Excuse me," the guest began, looking slightly irritated. "I need a different room."

Kristy cast a puzzled glance at April before turning back to the woman with a warm, professional smile. "Of course, ma'am. May I ask if there's a particular issue with your current room?"

"Simply put, it's freezing," the guest replied, rubbing her arms for emphasis. "I've tried adjusting the thermostat, but it doesn't seem to get warm enough. It just doesn't work."

April sympathized with the woman, knowing how important a comfortable room was to her guests, especially during the holidays. They would always try to ensure their guests were happy and comfortable. And if that meant changing the room, then they would give her a new room.

April leaned against the wall beside her, observing Kristy's interaction with the seemingly disgruntled guest. Her dark hair framed her face as she listened intently to the conversation unfolding before her.

"It is seriously unbearably cold," the guest complained, rolling her eyes for effect.

Kristy, ever the empathetic employee, looked genuinely concerned. "Of course! We'll get you situated right away."

As April watched, she wondered if something had gone awry with the furnace or the heater in the upstairs room where the guest was staying. But then it dawned on her – if there were any issue with the heating system, the entire house would be cold. And it wasn't.

So then what was wrong with this room? And could they really be able to find a warmer room when every part of the house was on the same heating system?

"Here you go," Kristy said, handing over a key to the guest with a reassuring smile. "This room is on the ground floor, right over there."

"Thank you," the guest replied, visibly relieved. Then, scanning the festive decorations adorning the walls and staircase, her nose crinkled in disapproval. "Is there anything you can do about these decorations, though? They're just too... Christmas-y. Too bright and obnoxious."

April stifled a chuckle at the woman's remark. The small town of Sandcrest had always been festive. If this woman wanted a less festive town, she could have gone anywhere else.

There wasn't a reason for her to take down her carefully thought out decor. They were simply red, green, white and blue. Sure, the colors were bright and some of the knick knacks were cheesy. But if anything, she thought her decorations were rather tasteful in comparison to the chaos and festivities of downtown.

"Unfortunately, we can't change the decorations," Kristy responded apologetically, her voice wavering slightly. "We want our guests to feel the warmth and joy of the holidays during their stay."

"Well, it's just too much," the guest muttered, eyeing up the lights strewn across the lobby. "It's distracting. There's no need for such nauseating decor."

April couldn't help but laugh as the guest continued her complaint about the Christmas decorations. The twinkling lights and festive garlands were a far cry from obnoxious in her opinion.

She glanced at Kristy, noticing the young woman's struggle to find a suitable response. Deciding to intervene, April stepped forward with a warm smile.

"Ah, I understand how you might feel," April said, her tone light and empathetic. "But it's just the Christmas season, and we want our guests to experience the festive atmosphere of the town. We're simply preparing for the holiday celebrations."

The guest rolled her eyes before snatching the key from Kristy's hand. "Well, at least you don't have one of those gaudy trees," she grumbled as she made her way across the polished wooden floor toward her new room.

As April watched the woman shuffle towards her new room, she felt a flicker of amusement – and perhaps just a touch of sympathy. It seemed that even in this idyllic small town, there would always be those who couldn't quite appreciate the magic of the season.

But April's laughter faded as the woman's words struck a chord. It was late in the season for picking up a tree.

With everything going on, the thought of a tree had nearly slipped her mind. Most people around town already had theirs up and ready. It was on her list of things to do, but the days seemed to be passing her by faster than she was ready for.

And now, with Jackson returning to town today, she was running out of time. She needed to find the perfect tree, not only to complete the festive decor but also to make the bed and breakfast feel like a true home for the holidays.

As the guest disappeared around the corner, April turned to Kristy, her eyes wide with urgency. "Kristy, would you mind holding down the fort for a bit? That woman reminded me I need to run into town and pick up a tree."

CHAPTER NINE

April's fingers gently brushed over the receptionist's desk, grabbing a handful of peppermints and her car keys before tossing them into her purse. Her heart danced with anticipation; she had always loved Christmas, and this year was no different. The scent of freshly brewed coffee wafted through the air as she glanced around the cozy bed and breakfast she had worked so hard to create.

"Mom!" Georgia's voice rang out, filling the room with its warmth. April looked up to see her daughter entering the house, cheeks flushed from the cold air outside, her wavy hair cascading down her back like a waterfall. Georgia's green eyes sparkled with excitement. "What's going on? Are you heading out?"

"Hi, sweetheart," April said, unable to hide the grin that spread across her face at the sight of her daughter's happiness. "I'm just about to go out and find us a Christmas tree."

"Really?" Georgia exclaimed, her face lighting up even more. "Can I come with you?"

April blinked in surprise, her mind racing as she tried to size up her daughter. It felt like ages since she'd been available to do something. The past week and a half she'd been down for Christmas break, she hadn't spent more than an hour at a time doing something together.

"Are you sure? Don't you have plans or something going on?"

"Nothing until later tonight," Georgia replied, shrugging off her coat and hanging it on the rack by the door. "I'd really love to look for a tree." Her eyes were soft and sincere.

"Of course!" April answered, her own eyes shining with unshed tears. "I would absolutely love that, hun." She hesitated for a moment, savoring the feeling of having her daughter by her side once again. "Give me just a second to grab my coat, and we'll head out."

As April reached for her coat, her thoughts raced with gratitude and happiness. She couldn't believe her luck – that after all this time, she would finally have the opportunity to share a special moment with her daughter. It was like a Christmas miracle in itself, one she wouldn't trade for anything.

"Ready?" Georgia asked, already bundled up near the door.

"Absolutely," April replied, her heart swelling with joy. "Let's go find us the perfect tree."

***

The sun glistened off the windshield as April and Georgia drove along the island's winding roads. Their laughter filled the car, mingling with the hum of the engine and the occasional Christmas song on the radio. As they passed a cluster of evergreens, April slowed down, her eyes scanning the sparse forest.

"Mom, I thought there'd be more trees than this," Georgia said, disappointment coloring her voice.

"Me too," April sighed, her fingers tapping against the steering wheel. "I heard there were some that naturally grew here, but it looks like we're out of luck."

"Can't we just get a fake tree?" Georgia suggested, raising an eyebrow. "It's easier and we'll probably find a prettier one in the store."

"True, but there's something about the smell and feel of a real tree that makes Christmas special," April explained, her gaze distant as she recalled childhood memories of decorating the family tree. "It's tradition to have a real one, and I want to keep that alive."

"Alright, fair enough," Georgia conceded, leaning back in her seat.

Determined, April steered the car off the island, heading towards a tree farm she had seen advertised. As they approached their destination, she glanced at her daughter, concern furrowing her brow. "What time are your plans tonight?"

"Four o'clock. But it's okay, I can push them back," Georgia replied, checking her phone.

April looked over at the clock and realized there was only ten minutes until four. She felt bad for spending so much time driving across the island searching for trees that had already been claimed and cut down.

"Are you sure?" April asked, guilt gnawing at her stomach as they pulled into the tree farm's gravelly lot. Her heart sank when she saw the meager selection before them – only a few scraggly trees remained, each looking more pitiful than the last.

"Positive," Georgia insisted, her eyes fixed on the sad display. "Let's see if we can find a tree that isn't too Charlie Brown-esque."

With a nod, April parked the car, and they stepped out into the crisp winter air. She tried to focus on their mission, but couldn't shake the feeling that she was taking precious time away from her daughter's plans.

April scanned the nearly barren lot, her heart sinking further with each passing moment. She spotted a worker in the distance, sweeping up the scattered needles and that littered the field.

"Excuse me!" she called out, waving him down. "Where are all your trees?"

The worker heaved a weary sigh as he approached them. "I'm afraid they've all been taken for the season," he explained, his voice tinged with apology. "We had quite the rush this year."

"Thank you," April replied, disappointment evident in her voice. Turning to Georgia, she suggested, "Let's try another place."

"Sure thing, Mom," Georgia agreed, though her tone lacked its previous enthusiasm.

As they drove to the next tree farm, April couldn't help but worry about the impact of their quest on her daughter's day. By the time they arrived at the second farm, only to find it completely devoid of trees, Georgia's frustration was palpable.

"Mom," she said carefully, "I'm just going to cancel my plans for tonight."

"Oh, hun," April began, "If we start heading back now, we can make it in time for you to go out."

"No, no," Georgia said with a slight grin. "It's alright. We came out to get a tree, we're going to get a tree."

April felt horrible for taking her daughter's time, but at least they were able to spend some time together. Georgia was clearly disappointed she missed her plans, which was understandable. But April was now determined to try and find that tree.

At the third tree farm they'd found, they finally came across an extremely limited selection of trees. The sight of the sparse options made April's heart heavy with guilt. "I'm really sorry you had to cancel your evening plans, Georgia."

"It's okay, Mom," Georgia insisted, though the slight quiver in her voice betrayed her disappointment. "Let's just find our tree."

Together, they walked through the tree farm, examining each potential candidate. Though the trees were far from perfect, April appreciated the effort Georgia put into the search. They discussed each and every option, trying to look at the positives of each imperfect tree.

The icy wind whipped through the tree farm, chilling April to her bones as she clutched the small saw in her gloved hand. Her breath fogged up in the air, and the surrounding trees swayed softly, their needles whispering a winter's melody.

"Hey, Mom, what about this one?" Georgia called out, her voice slicing through the cold air.

April turned to see her daughter standing next to a rather unassuming tree. It had short branches but appeared fuller than any of the others they had seen thus far. The top was slanted, though with a bit of effort, they might be able to straighten it out in the tree stand. She approached the tree, her footsteps crunching on the snow-covered ground, and smiled at Georgia.

She studied the tree, her eyes taking in its slanted top and somewhat lopsided shape. It was far from the stereotypical Christmas tree look, but perhaps it held a certain charm that could grow on them. "It might work," she conceded, hope flickering in her chest.

"Then let's take it home," Georgia said, offering her mother a small, genuine smile.

"I guess the least we could do is give it a shot," April agreed, determination sparking within her as she envisioned the tree adorned with twinkling lights and cherished ornaments.

"Alright, here goes nothing." Georgia rolled up her sleeves, ready to help her mother take on the challenge of cutting down their chosen tree.

Together, April and Georgia positioned themselves on opposite sides of the trunk, taking turns sawing through the thick bark. Their breaths came out in heavy pants as the saw bit into the wood, slowly creating a path that would set their tree free.

The saw drew back and forth. Back and forth. Back and forth.

It felt like they were making no progress. After seven full minutes of sawing, the tree had barely been sliced. "Are we using this thing wrong?" Georgia asked.

"No, I think we're just bad at this," April replied. "We just need to push harder. Put more pressure on it."

"We couldn't have gotten an axe or something easier?" Georgia asked, brows raised.

April chuckled. "No, this is all they had."

"Alright, fine. But next time, we're going to get a fancy electric saw, and we'll just buzz right through this trunk. This is exhausting, and I'm never doing it again."

Her daughter was dramatic, but also not wrong. It was incredibly hard with the saw in their hands, which must have been dull or something. Still, it was what they had in the moment. They kept pushing forward until finally, they began to see some progress.

"Almost...there..." Georgia grunted, her face flushed from exertion.

With one final, joint push, the saw tore through the remainder of the trunk, and the tree began to lean precariously. April and Georgia stepped back as it fell with a gentle thud onto the snow-dusted ground.

"Whew, we did it!" April exclaimed, wiping the sweat from her brow.

"Teamwork makes the dream work," Georgia joked, her green eyes sparkling with pride. Despite her earlier frustration, she seemed genuinely happy to have shared this experience with her mother.

As they lugged the tree back to their car, an employee of the tree farm approached and offered to help them secure it atop the vehicle. Grateful for his assistance, April thanked him profusely while Georgia made sure the knots were tight and secure.

"Ready for the trip home?" Georgia asked, closing the car door with a satisfying click.

"Absolutely," April replied, her heart warmed by their successful tree hunt, and the precious memory they had created together.

As April pulled onto the main road, she glanced over at Georgia, who was absentmindedly picking at a loose thread on her sleeve. The sun was beginning to dip below the horizon, casting a warm orange glow across the interior of the car. April smiled as she took in the sight of their hard-earned tree strapped securely to the roof.

"Georgia, I just wanted to say...I'm really glad we were able to do something together today," April said hesitantly, unsure of how her daughter would react. "It means a lot to me."

"Me too, Mom," Georgia replied softly, her gaze shifting from her sleeve to meet her mother's eyes. "Everything has been so busy lately, and it felt nice to take a break and spend some time with you."

April noticed the vague nature of Georgia's response, but chose not to pry. There was a reason Georgia had suddenly become so busy in town. She wasn't sure what it was yet, but maybe her daughter would tell her eventually.

She had learned from past experience that pushing too hard could lead to walls going up between them. Instead, she focused on the positive outcome of their day together.

"Finding this tree with you has made it even more special," April continued, her voice filled with warmth. "No matter how crooked or sparse it may be, we found it together, and that's what truly matters."

Georgia smiled, tucking a stray strand of her wavy hair behind her ear. "You're right, Mom. It'll be a great addition to the house. And everyone will appreciate the story behind it."

"Perhaps they will," April agreed, feeling a swell of pride for her daughter's creative spirit. "And who knows? Maybe this little tree will become a tradition for us, finding the most unique one each year."

"Eh, I don't know about that. It might be nice to get a solid, big tree next year. But I'm down for an adventure next year. Sounds like a plan to me," Georgia chuckled, her green eyes shining with amusement.

As they continued their drive home, the sky transforming into a stunning tapestry of reds and purples, April couldn't help but feel grateful for the day they had shared. It wasn't often that she and Georgia got to spend quality time together, and today felt like a gift.

Though she knew there were still many things left unsaid between them, April chose to cherish this moment, knowing that sometimes it was better to simply enjoy the present rather than trying to uncover every hidden truth.

CHAPTER TEN

April and Georgia stood before the majestic Christmas tree, their faces furrowed in concentration as they attempted to get it to stand straight in its stand. They'd set it in the middle of the lobby, beside the fireplace.

"Mom, try turning the screws on the left a bit more," Georgia suggested, her eyes squinting at the tree from the side. Her wavy long hair was pulled back into a messy bun to keep it out of the way as she worked.

"Alright, let's give that a try," April said, her medium length dark hair framing her face as she bent down and adjusted the screws as instructed by her daughter. She took a step back and placed her hands on her hips. She had to tilt her head to the side to examine the tree. "No, it still seems off."

"Let me take a look," Georgia said, switching places with her mother. After a few more adjustments and some gentle nudging, the tree finally stood tall and straight.

"Perfect!" April exclaimed, clapping her hands together with a smile. "Now we can start decorating."

Her expression fell as she took in the rest of the lobby. The warm glow from the twinkling lights felt dimmed, contrasting with the few empty spots on the walls where festive decorations once adorned the space.

"Kristy, what happened to the other decorations?" April asked, concern etched on her face. Kristy emerged from the kitchen, wiping her hands on a dish towel, a sheepish look in her eyes.

"Sorry, April," she said apologetically. "That guest who was complaining earlier wouldn't stop until I agreed to take some of the brighter décor down. She said it was too overwhelming for her."

April sighed, disappointment clouding her features. She had hoped to create a cozy and welcoming atmosphere for all her guests, especially with Jackson coming over soon. Noticing her mother's frustration, Georgia placed a reassuring hand on April's shoulder.

"Mom, the tree is going to be beautiful once we hang the ornaments. It'll make up for the decorations we had to take down," she said optimistically.

"You're right, Georgia," April agreed, her spirits lifting at the thought of the warm and intimate tree-decorating session they were about to share. "Let's get started."

April brushed a strand of her dark hair behind her ear as she reached for the box filled with ornaments. She glanced at Georgia, who was eagerly selecting glittering baubles from the assortment.

The sight of her daughter's excitement brought a smile to April's face, despite her disappointment. They were creating new memories in this small town, and that was something to cherish.

"Alright, let's start with these," Georgia announced, extending an armful of ornaments towards April.

"Perfect," April replied, taking a few from Georgia's grasp. "These will bring some much-needed Christmas spirit back into the room."

As they began hanging the ornaments on the tree, April couldn't help but steal glances at the front door. Jackson would be arriving any moment now, and her heart fluttered with anticipation. She wanted to see him walk through the door and embrace her.

Still, they rummaged through the ornaments, pulling them out one at a time and preparing to place some on the tree.

The sound of a knock on the door interrupted the sharing of memories and laughter that filled the lobby.

"Jackson, you don't need to knock! You're practically family," she called out as she crossed the room to open the door. However, instead of the familiar face of her ranch hand, she found herself looking at a stern-faced man holding an envelope.

"April Faith?" he asked, his voice gruff and uninviting.

"Um, yes. That's me," April replied, puzzled by the sudden intrusion.

"Consider yourself served," he stated flatly, handing her the envelope before turning on his heel and walking away.

April stood there, momentarily stunned by the encounter, clutching the packet of papers against her chest. Her previous excitement was quickly replaced with a growing sense of dread. What could she possibly be served for?

"Mom? Who was that?" Georgia called from across the room, concern lacing her voice.

"Uh, I'm not sure, honey," April answered hesitantly, her fingers trembling as she began to open the envelope. "I'll find out soon enough."

"Everything okay?" Georgia pressed, pausing in her decorating.

"Let's continue with the tree," April suggested, forcing a smile onto her face and hoping that whatever was contained within the envelope wouldn't ruin their evening. "Try to find that ornament you made when you were in elementary school."

Steeling herself, April pulled out the stack of papers from the envelope and began to skim through them. Her heart pounded as she read the words "City of Sandcrest" and "lawsuit" in bold at the top. She felt her stomach twist into knots as she realized what this meant.

She sat down behind the receptionist's desk and began to skim through the first few pages. It was paperwork she'd seen before, even written a hundred times. So she knew exactly where to look to get the information she wanted.

And she found it, though it didn't make her burden any lighter. If anything, it confused her.

The lawsuit as a whole was ridiculous. They were going to have a hard time proving any of their points in court. A judge would most likely rule in April's favor.

But then she thought about the truth behind the lawsuit. It was most likely Isaac that filed all of the paperwork, paid for the lawyers and put it in their heads that the city could win.

And Isaac was a very powerful man. He could be powerful enough to get a judge to side with him. While April knew law, she didn't know any of the local judges and what they were like. It was going to be hard to tell if she was heading into a fair fight.

Even with her legal expertise, it wouldn't be easy to win this battle, but she refused to let fear or doubt consume her. The future of her ranch – and her beloved horses – depended on her ability to fight back and protect what was hers.

The heavy oak door shut behind the stranger, leaving a lingering chill in the air. Georgia studied her mother's face, concern furrowing her brow as she ventured, "So, who was that guy?"

"Nothing to worry about," April replied, her voice wavering slightly. She tried to shove the thoughts of the lawsuit into the back of her mind, but they clung tenaciously, threatening to dampen the festive mood.

"Mom—" Georgia began again, reaching out toward the stack of papers in April's hands.

"Georgia, let's just—" April started to say, but the jingle of the front door interrupted her. The door swung open, and there stood Jackson, dusted with snowflakes like powdered sugar on a Christmas cookie. His blue eyes twinkled as he took in the scene before him.

"Jackson!" Georgia exclaimed, her green eyes lighting up. She rushed forward and enveloped him in a hug, her embrace warm and genuine. April smiled as she stepped closer, planting a tender kiss on his cheek as he shrugged off his coat.

"Wow, you ladies have really outdone yourselves this year," Jackson remarked, looking around at the sparkling decorations adorning the lobby. "It looks like a winter wonderland in here."

"Thank you," April said, her cheeks reddening slightly at his compliment. "We still have a tree to decorate, though, so feel free to join us."

"Sounds like fun," he agreed, rubbing his hands together to chase away the cold. "But first, who was that guy that just left? He didn't look too friendly."

April hesitated for a moment, her heart sinking as she considered revealing the truth. But casting a glance at the twinkling lights and the half-decorated tree, she whispered instead, "I'll tell you later, Jackson. For now, let's just focus on making this place as magical as possible."

"Alright," Jackson nodded, accepting her words without question. "Let's get to work, then."

As they gathered around the tree, April felt a rare sense of contentment settle over her. The troubles of the world may have been pressing in from all sides, but for now, she would cherish this moment - with her daughter and the man who meant more to her than she could ever express.

April clapped her hands together, a spark of inspiration lighting up her eyes. "How about some hot cocoa to keep us warm while we decorate the tree?"

"Sounds perfect, Mom," Georgia chimed in, excitement lacing her voice.

"Count me in," Jackson agreed, his eyes crinkling at the corners as he offered April a warm smile.

As she busied herself in the kitchen, the aroma of rich cocoa mingling with the scent of pine needles from the Christmas tree, April felt a flutter in her chest. She poured steaming hot cocoa into three festive mugs, topping each with a generous dollop of whipped cream and a sprinkle of cinnamon.

Returning to the living room, she handed the mugs to Georgia and Jackson, watching as they sipped their drinks and resumed their decorating duties.

"Careful with those lights, Georgia," April cautioned, noticing her daughter struggle with the tangled mess of twinkling fairy lights. "You don't want to break them."

"Got it, Mom," Georgia replied, nodding determinedly.

"Here, let me give you a hand," Jackson offered, reaching out to assist her.

Watching the two of them work together, April felt her heart swell with affection. Despite the uncertainty looming over the ranch, these were the moments that truly mattered – simple times shared with the people she loved most.

"Mom, where do you want this ornament?" Georgia asked, holding up a delicate glass bauble that glistened under the soft glow of the fairy lights.

"Right there looks good, sweetheart," April replied, pointing to a vacant spot on the tree.

"Perfect," Georgia murmured, gently securing the ornament in place.

As she observed the scene before her, April felt a curious mix of emotions. The joy of the Christmas season, the warmth radiating from Jackson's gentle presence, and the pride she took in her daughter's achievements were all tempered by the lingering worry for the future of the ranch.

"Everything alright, April?" Jackson asked, his perceptive gaze catching the flicker of concern in her eyes.

"Of course," she answered, forcing a smile onto her lips. "Just enjoying this moment with the two of you."

"Then let's make it a moment to remember," he said, raising his mug in a toast. "To the best tree decorating team in Sandcrest!"

"Cheers!" Georgia declared, clinking her mug against theirs.

In that instant, as they laughed and toasted together, April chose to embrace the happiness of the present, allowing herself to hope that, somehow, everything would work out in the end.

CHAPTER ELEVEN

April's eyelids fluttered open, the weight of her slumber anchoring them down like tiny sandbags. She groaned, her body feeling as if it had been entwined in battle with the mattress throughout the night.

She lay there, static, staring at the ceiling fan as its blades cut lazy circles through the morning air. Her limbs were slow to obey the commands of waking life, and she rolled out of bed with the grace of a toppled mannequin.

"Come on, April," she murmured to herself, voice husky with sleep as she padded across the cool wooden floor. The bathroom mirror greeted her with a reflection that seemed unfamiliar — dark hair tousled, eyes clouded with the remnants of dreams.

She methodically brushed her teeth, watching the paste foam and swirl down the sink in a minty spiral. The bristles through her hair felt like tiny soldiers putting order back into her disheveled world, and she dressed in soft layers, each garment a quiet promise to try to make the day better than its beginning.

Descending the creaking staircase, the ambiance of the bed and breakfast wrapped around her — an ambiance now plagued by the absence of the usual festive adornments. Her heart dipped slightly at the sight of bare spots where garlands and ribbons once hung, casualties of an unfortunate encounter with a particularly difficult guest.

But then, her gaze landed on the evergreen tree standing proudly in the corner of the lobby, its branches adorned with delicate baubles and twinkling fairy lights, a sentinel of Christmas cheer amidst the stripped decor.

"Could've been worse," she told the silent room. "At least you're still here."

As April approached the tree, her hand reaching for the plug of the lights, a sudden vibration in her pocket caused her to pause. She drew out her phone, the screen illuminating with the anticipation of a message received. Her thumb hesitated over the device, a knot forming in her stomach.

She tried to reassure herself, thinking maybe it was Georgia waking up and asking about breakfast. Or Jackson telling her good morning. With a tentative swipe, April opened herself up to whatever news awaited her, ready or not.

The notification on April's phone glinted like a shard of ice, the one-star rating stark against the backdrop of her otherwise stellar reviews. Her thumb trembled as she tapped to expand the comment, every lawyerly instinct tensing for a fight she never wanted in her newfound sanctuary.

"Absolutely appalling service," the screen accused in cold digital print. "A worker bellowed at us like we were children, and the owner—a woman with no hospitality—threw us out despite our confirmed reservation!"

April's breath hitched, a gasp of disbelief escaping her lips. None of it was true.

She sank into the nearest chair, wood creaking under the sudden burden of her dismay. The memory of each guest paraded through her thoughts—a slew of faces and names, some worn by time and others still fresh. She could recall their smiles, their stories shared over breakfast, the warm thank-yous as they departed, laden with memories.

If it was someone who had a bad experience, they would have stated their critiques. Why would they have to make something up? Why pretend like something else went wrong? It didn't make any sense.

The nice ones had written kind reviews. And the guests that had bad experiences were always treated with respect and understanding. No one had yelled at a guest, especially not April. She would never throw anyone out of the hotel.

With a heavy sigh, April pushed herself up and approached the tree again, its darkened form now a silhouette against the dawn's light creeping through the curtains. Her fingertips brushed against the plug, and for a moment, she hesitated, the chill of the review haunting her.

She knew she couldn't let it ruin her Christmas spirit. She was going to defy this begrudging person.

But as she finally pushed the plug into the outlet, a sharp click echoed through the lobby, followed by an abrupt plunge into darkness. The cheerful glow of the morning sun was swallowed by shadows as the lobby lights fizzled into nothingness.

"Perfect," April said dryly, the word tasting sour on her tongue. "Just perfect."

In the dimness, she stood motionless, a solitary figure enveloped by the quiet, contemplating the silence that now mirrored the blank spaces where reviews should shine with praise, not damaged by deceit.

The darkness around her felt like a tangible thing, wrapping her in a cloak of frustration, woven through with threads of confusion and helplessness. She'd done something to the fuse. The lights they'd carefully spread across the lobby were all out.

April's hands fumbled for the flashlight in the utility drawer, its beam cutting through the gloom as she made her way to the basement. She avoided the creaky fourth step, a mental note from countless trips down these wooden stairs.

The air grew cooler and mustier as she descended, the scent of old books and forgotten furniture mingling with her rising anxiety.

She just needed to find the right switch and flip it back on, right? It would be easy, she thought.

Her hand hovered over the breaker panel, a chaotic array of switches with no rhyme or reason. The labels had long faded or had been written in cryptic shorthand by some electrician who probably thought he'd remember what "GV" or "LL" meant decades on.

April thought it felt like defusing a bomb without the manual. She tried reading them, but wondered if guessing her way through her electric panel was the best idea. She didn't want to make things worse.

She had to squint to make out the warnings that danced just beyond the reach of clarity. It was all hieroglyphics to her – legal jargon she could translate in her sleep, but this? This was another language entirely.

Her phone, which she'd slipped into the pocket of her jeans, vibrated against her thigh, pulling her from the labyrinth of circuits and wires. With a reluctant sigh, she retrieved it, the screen casting an eerie light across her features.

She knew she had to call Jackson. He had experience with things like this. The electrical jargon would feel like actual words to him. She dialed his number and pushed call.

"Hey, Jackson. I'm... I'm sorry to bother you, but I'm at my wit's end here." Her voice was weary, the strain of the morning's events threading through each word.

"Hey, April. What's going on? I was planning on coming over later." Jackson's voice filtered through the line, warm and steady, a stark contrast to the cold shadows around her.

"The lights went out in the lobby. I think I've blown a fuse trying to make the Christmas tree look less pitiful. I'm standing here in the basement and—well, I'm having trouble making sure I know what to do. I can't mess it up again." April closed her eyes briefly, feeling the tightness in her chest ease just a smidge at the sound of his concern.

"Alright, take a deep breath for me, April. I'll be right over. Just sit tight, okay?"

"Thank you, Jackson. I really appreciate it," she replied, a small, genuine smile touching her lips despite the situation.

"Of course. I'm on my way." His assurance was a balm, and she felt a thread of hope weave through the tangle of her worries.

"See you soon," she said before hanging up, her fingers lingering on the end call button as if to draw out the momentary connection.

She pocketed her phone, her mind wandering back to the tangled mess of her morning. It wasn't just about the lights or the review; it was everything together. The lawsuit, the new relationship with Jackson, her daughter never home.

And now, in the heart of her bed and breakfast, wrapped in darkness, she realized that sometimes you need more than your wits and willpower.

Sometimes, you need your friends who can help you find the light again.

The hush of the darkened lobby was punctuated by the soft tread of Georgia's slippers as she descended the staircase, her green eyes wide with concern in the dim light filtering through the curtains.

"Mom?" Georgia's voice was a thread of worry weaving through the silence. "What happened to all the lights?"

April, perched on the edge of an armchair, felt the tension knotting between her shoulder blades. She looked up, her features etching a map of exhaustion. "I, well-" she began before being interrupted.

A vibration in her pocket cut through her confession like a sharp intake of breath. April's hand dove into her cardigan, retrieving the phone with a sense of foreboding. The screen illuminated her face, casting shadows that danced with the tremor of her fingers.

"Another one..." April mumbled, staring at the notification as if it were a portent of doom.

Georgia stepped forward, her wavy hair cascading over her shoulders as she leaned in to glimpse the cause of her mother's dismay. "Is everything okay?"

Without reading past the glaring one star that seemed to sear itself into her retina, April locked the phone and met her daughter's gaze. "Yes, but we have to talk. There's something going on," she said, her voice laced with the gravity of the situation. "Can you get Kristy, so we can come up with a plan?"

"Of course, I'll go tell her that you want to talk," Georgia replied.

"Meet me in the living room," April instructed, rising from the chair with a grace that belied her inner turmoil. "We need to figure out what's happening before it escalates."

As Georgia's footsteps receded, April allowed herself a moment to gather her thoughts. Her mind, once adept at constructing legal defenses, now grappled with the vulnerability of her new life. She had traded courtroom battles for cozy guest rooms, yet here she was, fighting a different kind of accusation.

She moved to the window, tracing the cold glass with a fingertip, watching as her breath fogged the pane. This house, with its warm memories and newfound dreams, was her sanctuary. But even sanctuaries could be besieged.

April was going to find a way out of this.

And with a quiet resolve, April turned and walked toward the living room where her family awaited, ready to face whatever storm was brewing outside the walls of their bed and breakfast.

CHAPTER TWELVE

The cozy lobby of the bed and breakfast hummed with a subdued tension, the couch bearing the weight of April and her impromptu council of troubleshooters. Dark hair framed April's determined face as she leaned forward, elbows on knees, addressing her small team.

"It's like we're under siege," she said, her voice carrying the cool, analytical edge honed from years in a courtroom. "Every corner we turn, there's another problem."

Georgia, lounging beside her mother, nodded, her long, wavy hair spilling over the back of the couch. Her green eyes, usually brimming with creative spark, now reflected concern. "Feels like someone's got it out for us."

Across from them, Jackson sat more upright than the rest, his light eyes scanning their faces, a quiet support amidst the chaos. His messy early morning hair gave him a wild, yet work-ready look, like he could step into any role needed at a moment's notice.

"If we split up today, we can each tackle one problem at a time," April concluded, glancing around at the faces that had come to mean so much in such a short time.

"Divide and conquer," Kristy chimed in, already poised on the edge of the seat, eager to act. Her energy was a welcome contrast to the heavy atmosphere weighing down the room.

As if summoned by their resolve, the crunch of gravel announced the arrival of another car. The four of them turned towards the window, watching as dust settled around the tires of the latest guest's vehicle.

"Looks like I'm up," Kristy declared with a determined smile. She sprang to her feet, smoothing her apron as she prepared to play her part in their plan. "I'll make sure these guests leave with nothing but praise."

"Thank you, Kristy. We need those good reviews now more than ever," April said, a grateful undertone threading through her words as she watched Kristy hurry to the receptionist's desk. The bell above the door tinkled its greeting, and Kristy's welcoming voice rose to meet the newcomers, her warmth genuine and unforced.

April's gaze lingered on Kristy, a beacon of hospitality, before turning back to Georgia and Jackson, who were already discussing their next moves. She felt a surge of pride – not just in the business she'd created, but in the people who stood by her, ready to defend this dream they all shared.

As Kristy's laughter mingled with the guests' pleased responses, April felt a flicker of hope. With each challenge, they grew stronger, their bond deepening. This bed and breakfast wasn't just a building; it was a home, a community, and a battleground they were determined to protect.

She sank back into the cushions, allowing herself a momentary breath. They would get through this, piece by piece, together.

The hush of the dimly lit lobby weighed heavily on April's shoulders as she turned to face Jackson. His light eyes, usually bright with a mischievous spark, now mirrored the same concern that had furrowed her brow. "Jackson," she began, her voice steady despite the unease coiling within her, "would you mind taking a look at the fuses? We can't have the guests stumbling around in the dark."

"Of course, April." Jackson rose smoothly from the couch, his movements calm and reassuring. His hand found hers, a fleeting touch that grounded her like an anchor in rough seas. "I'll get those lights back on before you know it." He leaned in, and his lips brushed against hers, a peck so swift yet tender, it left a warm glow that lingered far longer than the contact itself.

"Thank you," she whispered, watching as he disappeared into the shadows that led to the basement. A part of her longed to follow him, to escape into the quiet solidarity below. But duty beckoned, and the soft patter of Georgia's fingertips across her laptop keys drew her attention back to the immediate challenges at hand.

"Mom," Georgia said, her voice pulling April back from the precipice of worry, "let me dive into those reviews. Something about them doesn't add up, and I'm going to find out what." Georgia's eyes were fierce, her resolve unshaken by the chaos swirling around them.

April turned to her daughter, seeing not just the child she raised but the determined woman she was becoming. "That would be wonderful, Georgia." A small smile touched her lips, pride swelling in her chest. "As for me, I'll tackle the lawsuit. My law degree isn't gathering dust just yet."

"Go get 'em, Mom," Georgia encouraged, her gaze already scanning through a digital sea of falsehoods and slander.

April exhaled slowly, her thoughts turning inward as she prepared herself for the legal labyrinth ahead. Her fingers itched for the familiar texture of legal documents, the sharp tang of ink and paper. The lawsuit loomed large, its shadow threatening to swallow her dream whole, but she had fought battles in the courtroom before. She could do this too.

The papers would be a mess – chaotic, disorganized, formidable. Yet beneath her fear and frustration, there was a steeliness, a conviction honed over years of trials and tribulations, both personal and professional.

As much as her heart longed for love and the warmth of human connection, her mind was a weapon forged of logic and law. And amidst the storm of uncertainty, one truth remained clear: she would do whatever it took to protect her family, her home, and the animals who depended on her.

The sudden wash of warm light bathed the lobby in a welcoming glow, coaxing a sigh from April's lips. Jackson had fixed the electricity in the lobby. She welcomed the return of it like an old friend stepping through the door after a long absence.

For a fleeting moment, the weight on her shoulders seemed to lift, and she allowed herself the luxury of hope. With deliberate movements, she unfolded the paperwork across the expanse of the dining room table, papers whispering secrets as they settled into place.

Before her sat an overwhelming amount of legal language and ridiculous claims that could bring down her ranch. It was time to read through it all and look for some way to get out of this.

"Looks like we're back from the Dark Ages," Jackson's voice called out, his steps on the wooden staircase announcing his approach. A quick glance up, and April caught the tail end of his reassuring smile, the kind that had a habit of sending warmth cascading through her veins.

"Indeed," April responded, her fingertips tracing the edge of a document. "Thank you. That was quicker than I expected."

Jackson leaned against the doorway, his gaze flitting over the sea of papers before him. "I've got a knack for wrangling things, be it stubborn wiring or even more stubborn livestock."

"Speaking of which, I need to check on the horses, make sure they're set for the night." He scrubbed a hand through his tousled hair.

"Before I go," he said, shifting his attention back to her, "how's the mountain of legal jargon treating you?"

April pressed her lips together, considering the formidable stack before her. "Overwhelming," she admitted, her eyes not leaving the print that danced before her like a puzzle waiting to be solved. "But there's a path through this thicket somewhere. I just need to find it."

"Never doubted you for a second," he said with a quiet confidence that buoyed her spirits. "You've got this, April. If anyone can navigate through this, it's you."

"Appreciate the vote of confidence," she replied, her gaze lifting to meet his, seeking the sincerity she found reflected in his light eyes. It was a simple exchange, but it fortified her resolve like steel beams reinforcing a structure.

"Alright then, I'll leave you to it." Jackson pushed away from the doorframe, already mentally preparing for his next task. "Anything else before I head out?"

"No, that's all. Thank you, Jackson," April said, focusing once again on the documents as she heard his boots fade down the hallway. Her mind began to weave through legal clauses and stipulations, each sentence a thread in the tapestry of defense she was determined to create.

She could almost visualize the arguments, the counterpoints, the precise wording that might shield them from the storm brewing against them. The bed and breakfast was more than a business; it was a sanctuary, a testament to her resilience. Every line of text was a barrier, every signature a seal of protection. And she would stand guard over it all, her law degree a silent partner in this quiet battle for preservation.

"Find the loophole, April," she whispered to herself. "There has to be one." She turned the pagc, the dance of ink under lamplight, a familiar rhythm that steadied her heartbeat. There would be no surrender, not while she had breath in her body and law on her side.

April's fingers trembled ever so slightly as she turned another page of the hefty legal dossier. Her eyes, once the keen instruments that dissected courtroom arguments, now scanned the dense text for any semblance of hope.

The late afternoon sunlight filtered through the bay window, casting a warm glow over the paperwork sprawled before her like an unfurled map. Each document was a territory to navigate, each clause a potential path to victory or defeat.

A rustle at the entrance drew April's attention, and she looked up to find Georgia slipping into the room, her green eyes reflecting concern. "Mom, what have you found?" she asked, moving closer to the dining room table where the battle was laid out in ink and paper.

"Georgia," April began, her voice steady despite the storm brewing in her chest, "Isaac is trying to enforce a city ordinance to remove our horses from the ranch. It's a calculated move—if the city can rehome them, it'll be a huge task to get them back." She ran a hand through her dark hair, pushing away the strands that threatened to blind her vision.

Picking up a document, Georgia traced the bureaucratic language with her finger, her brows knitting together in concentration. "But we're still processing the refuge status, right? That should buy us time."

"Exactly," April confirmed, heartened by her daughter's grasp of the situation. "But it's a temporary shield at best. But so is this lawsuit. We're both just trying to buy time until we can officially win." She gestured towards a stack of forms yet untouched. "I must file a response immediately, try to settle this without stepping foot in court."

"Because of Isaac's influence?" Georgia leaned against the table, her creative mind clearly piecing together the harsh realities of their predicament.

"Sadly, yes. He might have friends in high places—judges included." April reached for a pen, its weight a familiar comfort in her hand. "We need to keep this battle out of court if we can."

Georgia placed a supportive hand on her mother's shoulder, a silent pillar of strength. "It sounds awfully complicated. But I know you can do it, Mom. You've always fought for these horses, for all of us, really." Her voice was a soothing balm, and for a fleeting moment, April allowed herself to absorb the pride in her daughter's words.

"Complicated has never stopped us before," April said, offering a small smile, though her heart raced with the uncertainty of their future. "And I won't let it now. These horses depend on us." Her resolve crystallized as she began to fill out the first of many forms, each a volley in the quiet war they waged.

"Let me know how I can help," Georgia insisted, her gaze unwavering. "I'm here for you, for the horses... for our home."

"Thank you, sweetheart." April's voice was soft but fierce. "Right now, this is where I wage the fight. But knowing you're with me—that's the true strength behind every word I write."

Her daughter smiled and took a seat beside her. She pulled out her laptop and set it gently on the table before opening it and beginning a presentation of her own.

Georgia's fingers danced across her keyboard with a rhythmic tapping that filled the silence of the dimly lit dining room. April watched, her brow furrowed, as her daughter's green eyes scanned the laptop screen with an intensity that mirrored her own in the courtroom.

"Well, I've found something on my end," Georgia said, her voice tinged with a mix of disbelief and frustration. "These bad reviews... they're not just random unhappy guests."

April leaned in closer, her gaze flitting over the glowing screen to see a list of usernames next to scathing critiques. Each one cut deep—not just as an owner but as someone who'd poured her heart into every corner of this establishment.

"Look at this." Georgia pointed at the dates. "These accounts were made recently, and they've only left one review—the ones dragging us down."

April absorbed the evidence, her former lawyer's mind piecing together the implications. "So, you're saying none of these people have actually stayed here?"

"Exactly." Georgia nodded emphatically. "It's all fabricated. No overlap with our guest logs or anything. It's like someone's going out of their way to target us."

The words hung in the air, a specter of malice that seemed to seep into the cozy warmth of the bed and breakfast. April felt the weight of each false accusation, knowing well the power of words to build or destroy.

She sighed, a heavy, world-weary exhalation that carried more than just her breath—it bore the burden of her struggles, the fight for her home, her livelihood, and now her reputation.

"Okay," she murmured, more to herself than to Georgia, "the only thing I can do is respond to these reviews. Professionally. Kindly." The taste of the words was bitter, like swallowing medicine she knew would sting on the way down.

"Are you sure?" Georgia asked, her eyebrows knitting together with concern. "You don't have to dignify those lies with a response, Mom."

April's hands hovered over the laptop before taking it gently from Georgia. Her fingers hesitated over the keys, each one a potential weapon or shield. "No, sweetheart, it's what has to be done. Ignoring them could ruin us. And fighting them would be even worse, and we can't afford that—not now."

Her mind raced with retorts and defenses, yet she carefully crafted replies that exuded nothing but grace under fire. With each word typed, she reaffirmed her commitment to the sanctuary she had built, a testament to her resilience.

"Thank you for digging into this," April said, glancing up at Georgia, whose presence was both comforting and empowering. "This might not be the battlefield I chose, but if it's where the fight finds me, I'll stand my ground."

Georgia reached over, squeezing her mother's hand, a silent vow of solidarity. And as April continued typing, her responses a delicate dance of diplomacy, there was a quiet determination set in her jaw—a promise that no matter the adversity, she'd face it head-on, with the poise of a woman who had already weathered many storms.

CHAPTER THIRTEEN

April's fingers were weary from sorting through the weighty paperwork, her eyes tracing over the legalese that threatened to blur into an indecipherable code. She had been a lawyer once, but the small-town life promised a simpler existence, away from the relentless lawsuits and cold courtroom battles. With the last form slotted into its designated folder, she leaned back, the satisfying snap of the binder closed like a period at the end of a taxing sentence.

The evening sun poured through the dining room windows, casting long shadows across the antique table where legal woes had sprawled in disarray just moments ago.

April raked her hands through her dark hair, the strands a cascading curtain of respite from the day's demands. She was ready to turn her attention to the renovation plans for her future bed and breakfast when a pair of gentle arms enveloped her from behind.

"Enough with the numbers and clauses for today, April." Jackson's voice was a soothing balm, his breath warm against her neck. "You need a break."

She could feel the tension melting under the pressure of his touch, the knots in her shoulders unfurling like the petals of a flower greeting the dawn.

"Jackson," she murmured, a small laugh escaping her lips as she turned to face him, finding those light eyes that always seemed to hold secrets she yearned to uncover. "What do you have in mind?"

"An official first date," he said, the corner of his mouth lifting into a lopsided smile that never failed to quicken her pulse.

"An official first date?" Surprise flickered across April's features, a spark of excitement igniting within her chest. She hadn't expected this—hadn't dared to hope—but here it was, a new chapter beckoning.

"Give me ten minutes," she breathed out, already making her way toward the stairs, the promise of something more calling her forward.

Jackson was waiting by the front door, the evening casting a soft glow over his short, messy hair. April descended the stairs, feeling the flutter of butterflies in her stomach. She had chosen a simple yet flattering dress, her anticipation manifesting in the choice of colors that complemented her dark hair.

"We're going to Giant's," Jackson announced as she reached the bottom step, his casual tone disguising the significance of the destination.

"Giant's?" The name conjured memories she thought she had filed away along with her past life. Nigel worked there; her ex-boyfriend Nigel.

"Best food in town, they say," Jackson continued, oblivious to the sudden shift in her demeanor. "I haven't had the chance to try it yet. Besides, didn't you say you ended things on good terms with Nigel?"

"Good terms, yes," April replied, her voice betraying none of the unease that tightened her chest. She wasn't sure if revisiting a place so entwined with her previous life was wise, but she trusted Jackson. His kindness was a compass that had yet to steer her wrong.

"Strange as it may seem, let's go," she said with a resolve that surprised even herself. This was about them, not the ghosts of relationships past. And if Jackson was willing to lead, she was ready to follow.

Hand in hand, they stepped out into the twilight, the door closing behind them with the gentlest click—a sound that, to April, signified the start of something new.

The clamor of Giant's greeted them like an old friend, a cacophony of chatter and the metallic symphony of kitchenware. April took in the familiar scent of grilled delicacies mingling with the subtle tang of lemony polish from the wood. It was a place where memories were dressed as waiters, serving up slices of the past.

"Here we are," Jackson said, his voice a grounding presence amidst the din. He led her through the maze of tables with a confidence that made her feel like they were the only two people in the room.

When they reached their table, nestled in a cozy corner, he pulled out her chair with the grace of a man who understood the silent language of chivalry. "For you," he smiled, eyes catching hers in a dance of unspoken affection.

"Thank you." April's words felt small against the warmth of his gesture. She sat down, smoothing the fabric of her dress beneath her. The soft glow of the candle on the table cast a golden sheen over Jackson's features as he complimented her, "You look beautiful tonight, April."

"Jackson, you're too kind," she replied, tucking a loose strand of her dark hair behind her ear, a blush creeping onto her cheeks. The way he looked at her made her heart flutter like a caged bird eager for flight.

Their conversation flowed like a gentle stream, touching on everything from the weather, which had been changing quickly, to the quaintness of the town. April found herself laughing more freely than she had in months, the laughter bubbling up from a wellspring of joy she hadn't realized was there.

"Seems like you're really settling into this new life here," Jackson remarked, admiration lacing his tone.

"It feels right, like I'm finding pieces of myself I didn't know were missing," April confessed, her voice barely rising above the surrounding bustle.

At the adjacent table, a server with a waterfall of chestnut curls woven into a tight braid attended to a demanding couple. She moved with a poised elegance, balancing plates and glasses with an effortless elegance. April couldn't shake the feeling of familiarity as she watched the woman jot down orders with a flourish.

As the server turned away from the neighboring patrons, her gaze met April's, and for a fleeting moment, a shadow crossed her face—a look not quite of recognition but something sharper, like the prick of a thorn. April's breath hitched slightly, the server's glare cutting through the warm atmosphere.

"Is everything alright?" Jackson asked, noting the change in her expression.

"Uh, yes, I just thought..." April trailed off, trying to shake the unsettling sensation. Her instincts honed from years of reading jurors told her the woman's animosity wasn't imagined. But she refused to let it dampen the evening, turning back to Jackson with a determined smile, "It's nothing. Tell me more about your ranch back home."

"Sure," Jackson said, though his eyes still held a flicker of concern. "But if anything is bothering you, you know you can tell me, right?"

"Of course," she reassured him, reaching across the table to briefly squeeze his hand. The simple touch sent a warmth through her that no spilled beer or icy glare could cool. Tonight was about them, and April was intent on keeping it that way.

Or at least, she thought she was. Until the server returned and stared at April over her shoulder. She couldn't ignore it much longer. She needed to know if she was going crazy or if this woman really had it out for her somehow.

The clinking of silverware and the low hum of conversation enveloped April as she tried to focus on Jackson's tales of upcoming ranch work, yet her attention kept darting back to the woman. Her intuition was a quiet drumbeat in her chest, signaling that something was amiss.

"Jackson," April whispered, her voice barely rising above the din, "could you look at something for me? Slowly, please."

Curiosity flickered across his features before he complied, turning just in time to catch the empty space where the server had been. "What am I looking for?"

April frowned, feeling slightly foolish. "There was a woman, a server. It's silly, but I felt like she was glaring at me—like she had something against me."

"April," Jackson said gently, with a small chuckle, "I doubt there's a soul in this town capable of disliking you. You're too kind, too genuine." His words seemed to wrap around her like a comforting blanket.

A flush crept up April's cheeks, and she rolled her eyes even as her heartbeat slowed. "You're just saying that because you're stuck working for me."

"Stuck? Or lucky?" He winked, and their laughter mingled with the restaurant's lively atmosphere.

Their drinks arrived, dewy glasses promising refreshment. April took a sip, allowing the cool liquid to calm her lingering unease. The burgers followed shortly after, hearty and aromatic, served up with a side of Jackson's infectious grin.

"Hey, I'm going to run to the bathroom. Be right back," Jackson said, pushing back from the table with an apologetic smile, heading towards the restrooms.

Alone, April allowed herself a moment to admire the way his jeans fit just right, how his light eyes sparkled with unspoken stories. But before she could indulge further, motion caught her eye—the same server, balancing a tray of beers close by. In a swift, fluid motion that belied accident, one of the frosty glasses tipped and doused April's lap with its contents.

"Oops," the server muttered, not quite meeting April's startled gaze. "Sorry about that."

"Sorry?" April sputtered, the cold shock registering in her mind as she dabbed uselessly at her soaked dress with napkins. The server, however, offered no help, already retreating with a hollow apology hanging between them.

Jackson returned to find April standing, a wet patch blooming across her dress, her expression a mix of disbelief and embarrassment. "April, what happened?" he asked, his brows knitting together in concern.

"It seems I've become a magnet for misfortune," she replied, trying to force levity into her voice despite the chill seeping into her skin.

"Let me help you," Jackson insisted, moving to her side.

"Thank you," April murmured, her thoughts a tangled mess. Was it truly an accident? Or was there more to the server's actions—a story untold, a grudge hidden behind veiled hostility? She pushed the questions aside, focusing instead on the kindness of the man beside her.

"I'm so sorry," Jackson said softly, retrieving a handful of napkins from the dispenser. He dabbed at the spreading dampness on April's dress, his touch cautious, as if afraid of causing her more distress.

"Jackson, this is..." April began, but found herself unable to finish. Her heart hammered against her ribs—not from the cold beer soaking through her clothes, but from the proximity of this man who had become a steady presence in her life.

"Unbelievable," he finished for her, his voice laced with indignation. "You shouldn't have to deal with this on what was supposed to be a pleasant evening."

She glanced up at him, noting the furrow between his brows and the earnest concern in his light eyes. The warmth in those eyes did something to soothe the icy discomfort on her skin. "I think I'd like to leave," she admitted, the words escaping on a tremulous breath.

"Let's get you cleaned up first." Jackson guided her toward the ladies' room, standing guard outside the door as she attempted to blot out the worst of the stain under the harsh fluorescent lighting.

Alone, she leaned heavily against the cool tile wall. This was not how she had envisioned her first date with Jackson—stained, slightly humiliated, and shivering in a bathroom.

"April?" Jackson's voice filtered through the door, tinged with worry. "Are you okay?"

"Almost ready," she called back, straightening her posture and squaring her shoulders. She wouldn't let this incident mar the entire night. Taking a deep breath, she stepped out, finding Jackson's gaze immediately locking onto hers.

"Better?" he asked, though his expression clearly conveyed that he was worried for her.

"Let's just forget this ever happened," April suggested, attempting to wrestle a smile onto her lips.

"Agreed. How about we get out of here and find something else to do with our time?" Jackson offered his arm, a gesture so chivalrous it nearly chased away the remnants of April's irritation.

"Sounds like a splendid idea," she replied, looping her arm through his with a grateful squeeze.

As they walked together towards the exit, she allowed herself the comfort of his support, the evening's earlier promise now cloaked in the reality of spilled beer and unspoken questions.

CHAPTER FOURTEEN

The early evening cast a soft, golden glow over the cobbled streets of the small seaside town, reflecting off the colorful shop windows and twinkling Christmas lights strung overhead.

April shivered as a gust of wind swept in from the sea, carrying with it the briny scent of saltwater and the distant call of seagulls. A chorus of carols floated on the air, mixing with the laughter of families.

"Here, you look like you could use this more than me," Jackson said, unwinding his thick woolen scarf from around his neck with those capable ranch hand fingers and draping it over April's shoulders. The fabric was warm from his skin and carried a hint of cedar and leather, a scent she'd come to associate with safety and comfort.

"Thank you," she replied, her teeth no longer chattering enough to compete with the jingle of bells coming from a nearby store. She smiled up at him, grateful for the gesture and the warmth it brought.

They continued their stroll, the setting sun painting the sky in hues of lavender and peach, blending seamlessly with the festive decorations. The town had outdone itself this year, with every lamp post wrapped in garlands and red ribbons, and the shop windows boasting scenes straight out of a storybook.

"Hey, my sister called earlier," Jackson said with a mischievous twinkle in his light eyes. "She and the little guy can't stop talking about you. They're already asking when they can see you again."

"Really?" April was genuinely flattered. An unexpected warmth bloomed within her chest, one that wasn't entirely from the scarf now snug against her neck. "I had such a lovely time with them. They have a beautiful home. And your nephew is absolutely adorable."

"He's a rascal, alright. Takes after his uncle, I guess." His grin was wide and infectious, causing her own lips to curve in response.

They laughed together, an easy, comfortable sound that mingled with the whispers of the ocean. April felt something inside her unfurl, a feeling she thought had been packed away. It was delight—simple and pure.

"He certainly is. He tried to tell me that the reindeer can fly because of the magic corn at the north pole." April said, remembering the little boy.

"Magic corn, eh? I'd better get some of that for the horses back at the ranch. Imagine the money we'd make if we had flying ponies," Jackson quipped, his chuckle resonating in the crisp evening air.

"Or the trouble you'd be in for scaring the neighbors," she teased back, her gaze locked with his, enjoying the sparkle in his eyes that seemed to mirror the Christmas lights.

"Trouble's my middle name," he said, leaning closer with a playful smirk.

"Is that so, Mr. Trouble?" she whispered, the proximity sending a shiver down her spine that had nothing to do with the chill.

"Only on days ending with 'y'," he replied, his breath a warm whisper against her cheek.

April's heart fluttered like the delicate wings of a butterfly caught in a gentle breeze. This connection with Jackson—it was tentative and new, yet it promised the kind of depth she hadn't known she was seeking.

Though unwelcome, her mind contrasted this slow-building flame to the firework that had been her relationship with Nigel, bright and fast, burning out before it ever really warmed her.

But this—this felt like the start of something enduring.

April's fingers traced the soft wool of Jackson's scarf around her neck, the fabric carrying a hint of his earthy scent mixed with the crisp sea air. They continued their stroll down the cobbled streets.

"Georgia really took to you," April said, tucking a dark strand behind her ear. "I was honestly surprised."

Jackson chuckled, his breath visible in the cold air. "Well, I'm not all that bad, am I?" His eyes crinkled with amusement as he nudged her playfully.

She laughed, but there was a thoughtful undertone to it. "No, it's not that. It's just... after the divorce, I didn't know how she'd react to me dating again. We had a happy little family and then it probably looked like I up and left."

She paused, watching a family laugh as they struggled to balance an overlarge Christmas tree. "But she's been so kind about it. She understands more than I thought she would. She's actually okay with me seeing someone else, which I wasn't sure would ever happen. Georgia's a hard lady to impress."

They passed a shop window where model trains chugged around a miniature winter village. Jackson paused, peering into the display before turning back to April. "It means a lot to me that Georgia approves. She's sharp—got a good head on her shoulders."

"Thank you," April replied, touched by his sincerity. "She's always had a knack for seeing people. A good judge of character."

"Seems like she gets that from her mom." Jackson's gaze held hers, steady and warm. He took a step closer, brushing his hand against hers. "Georgia's a great kid. Smart, creative. I like hanging out with her. Shame she's off at college, though."

"Tell me about it." April sighed, feeling the pang of absence. "But she loves what she's studying—interior design. It's her passion. She almost quit before coming here and learning she really loved design."

"Passion's important." Jackson's voice dropped to a more reflective note. "I spent too many years ignoring mine, chasing things that didn't matter. But now, working on the ranch, caring for the animals—it's where I'm meant to be."

Watching him speak, April saw the depth of his conviction, the quiet strength in his stance. She knew what it was to chase a life that didn't fit, remembered too well the confines of courtrooms and legal briefs.

Now, here in this town, with the sea's endless song and the company of a man who understood the value of simple joys, she began to truly appreciate the contours of a life reshaped by choice rather than expectation.

"Coming back to the land, to the animals—it must've felt like coming home," shc said softly, her heart swelling with a sense of kinship.

"Exactly." Jackson's smile reached his light eyes, making them sparkle. "Took me a while to find my way back, but I'm right where I want to be."

"Sometimes the longest journeys are the most necessary ones," April mused, her own journey reflecting in his words.

"Couldn't agree more," he said, giving her hand a gentle squeeze.

In the shared silence that followed, April felt the echo of unspoken understandings pass between them, the intermingling of past hardships and hopes for the future painting a picture more vivid than the festive scenes in the shop windows. It was a tapestry woven of new beginnings and second chances—a design she was only now starting to see take shape.

The air was filled with the scent of pine and saltwater. April's cheeks were rosy from the bracing wind that swept through the narrow lanes.

It was nice to see Jackson beginning to open up to her. She'd been waiting to see under the mysterious facade he'd showed her after meeting each other. This was exactly why she was falling for him. There was so much more than met the eye.

"Quite the charmer this town becomes during the holidays," Jackson remarked, his voice nearly lost to the playful gusts.

"It's magical," April replied, her breath forming small puffs of white cloud as she spoke.

She glanced at him, finding his eyes already on hers, and there was something in that gaze that made her heart skip just slightly. "You know, listening to you talk about your dreams...it’s refreshing,” she said, her voice tinged with earnest admiration. “You’ve got such a genuine soul, Jackson."

He chuckled lightly, his hands finding their way into his coat pockets. "Well, I've had my share of detours, but I'm glad I ended up here with you."

April felt a flush of pleasure at his words—this growing connection between them was tender, yet undeniable. With Jackson, it was like watching the dawn break slowly, the light intensifying with each passing moment.

"Jackson, I—" she began but was interrupted by the sudden splatter of raindrops, sharp and unexpected, that descended upon them.

"Woah!" Jackson exclaimed as they both began to feel the chilling water hit their skin, sharing a laugh as they began to get drenched.

"Come on!" He caught her hand and pulled her along, laughter trailing them like a kite tail, until they ducked under the protective awning of a nearby store. Its window display, a miniature village aglow with tiny fairy lights, reflected the surprise and delight in their eyes.

"Seems like the weather wanted to join our conversation," April joked, water droplets glittering in her dark hair like jewels.

"Maybe it did," Jackson agreed. His gaze lingered on her lips, and then, as if drawn by an irresistible force, he stepped closer, closing the gap between them.

"April, I—" he whispered, but no more words were needed. In the next instant, his lips met hers in a kiss that seemed to stop time, the rain's steady drumming creating a cocoon around them.

The world outside the awning blurred into insignificance as they held each other close, savoring the warmth that spread through them despite the chill of the rain.

In that embrace, April felt something solidify—a sense of belonging, a promise of tomorrows shared. She clung to him, letting the kiss deepen, aware that this was the beginning of something real and profound.

As they finally parted, breathless and smiling, April knew without a doubt that the path ahead was one she was meant to walk, with Jackson by her side.

CHAPTER FIFTEEN

Golden flecks of sunlight dappled the path as April walked to Alice's house, her hair swaying gently with each step. She couldn't help but think back to her first date with Jackson. The soft glow of candlelight had danced in his light eyes, and his short, messy hair seemed like a halo in the dimness of the evening.

They had laughed easily, the air around them charged with a promise of something more. But the sweetness of that memory was quickly soured by the bitter taste of her current predicaments.

As she walked, the fallen leaves crunched underfoot, their russet tones mirroring the tumultuous thoughts tumbling through her mind. The lawsuit lodged against her fledgling bed and breakfast was a thorn in her side, and the recent spate of bad reviews felt like personal attacks against the dreams she harbored for her new life in this small town—a stark contrast to her former world of legal battles and city lights.

"April, darling, you made it!" Alice's voice broke through her reverie as she crossed the threshold into the warm embrace of her friend's cozy living room.

"Wouldn't miss it for the world," April replied, offering a smile that didn't quite reach her tired eyes.

Alice led her to where Beth and Kellie were already seated, wine glasses in hand, ensconced in the plush comfort of deep armchairs. The familiar scent of mulled wine mingled with the cinnamon-spiced candles flickering on the mantelpiece, a sensory balm to April's frayed nerves.

"Here, take this." Alice handed her a glass, the crimson liquid swirling invitingly. "You look like you could use it."

"Thanks." April took an appreciative sip, feeling the warmth spread through her, loosening the knots of tension one by one.

"Can you believe Christmas is almost here?" Beth bubbled with excitement, her cheeks rosy from the glow of the fire and perhaps the wine. "I've been planning on what to get everyone. It's going to be so much fun!"

April shifted uncomfortably, the edge of guilt pricking at her conscience. Between the bed and breakfast and legal woes, she had forgotten again about gifts for her friends. "That's really sweet of you, Beth. I haven't had the chance to think about Christmas gifts yet."

"Nor have I," admitted April, setting her glass down on a coaster with a gentle clink. "And honestly, I wasn't planning on anything grand. Just... it's been a lot, you know?" Her gaze drifted to the flicker of the candles, their light reflecting the turmoil she felt within.

"Hey, it's okay. We all understand," Alice reassured her, reaching out to give her hand a comforting squeeze. "The important thing is we're together. Right?"

"Right," echoed April, a genuine smile finally breaking through as she leaned back into the cushions, surrounded by the warmth of friendship and the soothing clink of wine glasses. For now, the trials that awaited her outside these walls could wait. Here, she found respite—a temporary shelter from the storm.

Kellie’s confession hung in the air like a delicate snowflake, poised on the brink of dissolving. "Honestly, I wasn't going to get gifts this year," she said, her voice a low murmur against the backdrop of holiday melodies playing softly from Alice's vintage stereo. "But now, I don't want to be the only one showing up empty-handed. Would you guys be disappointed if I didn’t bring a gift for everyone?"

The statement sparked a flutter of dissent that danced through the room. Beth frowned slightly, her brow knitting as she contemplated the pile of unwrapped presents hidden away in her closet. "I thought we all loved our gift exchanges," she countered, her words laced with a gentle reproach.

"Of course we do, but it's a bit much, isn't it?" Alice chimed in, her fingers tracing the stem of her wine glass. "Getting a little something for everyone... it can get overwhelming."

April watched the exchange unfold, her chest tightening as if the garland draped around the room was constricting. The very idea of shopping for individual gifts felt like a weight pressing down upon her already burdened shoulders.

"It's a bit much to get everyone a gift, but it's nice to know that we all care," April said, putting in her own thoughts.

The ladies began to chatter, voicing their own opinions and thoughts. Their voices filled the room until there wasn't space for anything else.

"Wait, what about a Secret Santa?" Alice proposed, her eyes glinting with a solution. "We each get a name, and that's the only person we buy for."

"Secret Santa?" April repeated, the phrase rolling off her tongue like a welcomed elixir. The tension in her muscles ebbed away as she imagined the simplicity of it – one gift, one friend, no avalanche of expectations.

"Exactly!" Alice's enthusiasm was contagious. "It keeps the spirit alive without the stress."

April leaned forward, her elbows resting on her knees as she absorbed the proposition. The flickering candlelight painted shifting patterns on her face, mirroring the dance of thoughts behind her dark eyes. A single gift. She could manage that, couldn't she?

"Let's do it," she finally declared, her voice steady and certain. "Secret Santa sounds perfect."

"Agreed," Kellie added, relief softening her features.

"Okay, then," Beth conceded, though her tone carried a hint of reluctance akin to parting with a cherished tradition.

"Brilliant!" Alice beamed, already moving to fetch slips of paper from her desk.

As Alice scurried away, April let out a breath she hadn't realized she'd been holding. This was more than just a compromise on Christmas gifting; it was the alleviation of an invisible burden.

She didn't need to peruse endless shelves or online catalogs for the right scarf, the best kitchen gadget, or the trendiest home decor. Instead, she could focus on finding one perfect present for whoever's name graced the slip of paper she would draw.

"Here we are." Alice returned, distributing the folded squares among them. "No peeking until everyone has theirs."

April's fingertips grazed the coarse texture of the paper, a tangible representation of the upcoming holiday. It held potential, a mystery yet to unfold. She closed her hand around it, feeling its edges press into her palm, a small but significant promise of joy amidst the chaos of her world.

All of the ladies looked at their papers before tucking them into their purses. They all agreed not to spill who they had to anyone else in the group. With such a small name pool, they would be able to figure out who had who if even one person told.

The warmth of the room enveloped April as she nestled deeper into the plush armchair, her fingers curling around the stem of a wine glass. Soft laughter like tinkling chimes filled the space between the clinking of glasses and the rustle of movement. The comforting scent of cinnamon from a flickering candle mingled with the rich aroma of red wine, creating an atmosphere that was both festive and familiar.

"Alright, now that we've got the Christmas gifts all sorted," Beth announced, leaning forward with a conspiratorial glint in her eye, "I've got some juicy news to share."

April perked up, her curiosity piqued. She watched as Beth swirled her wine with an air of drama.

"There's a new girl working over at Giant's," Beth divulged, her voice dropping to a whisper even though the four of them were alone in Alice's cozy living room.

"Really?" April interjected, her mind flashing back to a brief encounter the day before. "I saw someone new there the other day." She bit her lip, wondering about the stranger who had seemed so out of place amid the usual bustle of the small grocery store.

"Yep," Kellie chimed in, setting her glass down on the coffee table. "Heard through the grapevine at the café that she came to our little island chasing after some man." A mischievous smile played on her lips.

Alice let out a chuckle, shaking her head. "Oh, to be young and foolish again." Her eyes twinkled with good-natured humor, and she reached for another piece of chocolate from the assortment on the table.

April's thoughts drifted, unbidden, to the woman's cold gaze that had briefly met hers across the aisles of canned goods and fresh produce. There was something unsettling about the way her presence had felt, like a sudden drop in temperature.

"I don't know, she didn't seem very friendly. Actually, it seemed like she had it out for me. She kept glaring and then she spilled a drink in my lap," April confessed, her voice trailing off as she recalled the sharpness in the woman's eyes.

"April, it's probably all in your head," Beth reassured her, waving a hand dismissively. "You're one of the most liked people around here. Everyone loves you."

"Exactly," Alice agreed, nodding emphatically. "I can't imagine anyone not taking to you."

"Maybe she was just having a bad day," Kellie suggested, her eyebrows knitting together in empathy. "You know how it is when you spill something—"

"She practically threw the beer into my lap," April interrupted, the memory surfacing with crystal clarity. "It felt intentional."

"Come on, April," Alice said, her tone light but her eyes searching April's face for signs of jest. "Who would deliberately spill a drink on our local sweetheart?"

"Maybe she's just clumsy," Beth offered, her voice tinged with doubt.

Yet, as the laughter and conversation flowed around her, April couldn't shake the uneasy feeling in her gut. The brief exchange with the newcomer replayed in her mind, casting a shadow over the jovial mood. It was more than just an accident; the look of disdain was too pointed, too personal.

"Still," April murmured, mostly to herself, "why would she take an instant dislike to me?"

The room fell silent for a moment, the weight of her words hanging in the air. Then, almost instinctively, the friends rallied around her with assurances and gentle teasing, their bond a bulwark against any brewing storm outside their circle of trust.

But deep down, April knew she needed to find out what this woman had against her. And she would probably have to do it alone.

CHAPTER SIXTEEN

April's fingers danced across the keys of her old typewriter, the rhythmic clack resonating through the spacious kitchen that doubled as her makeshift office. As she pulled the finished letter from the machine, her dark hair fell gently over her shoulder, partly obscuring the determined glint in her eyes. She read over the words, each one a strategic placement, a chess piece on the board of legal battle.

"*Dear City Council,*" it began, the script formal yet tinged with an undercurrent of surrender. "*It is with a heavy heart that I request a meeting to discuss the terms of a settlement...*" April continued to recite, her voice trailing off as she contemplated the city's relentless pursuit against her dream of taking care of the horses native to the island.

"*I would prefer to have a meeting outside of the courts at this time. A legal battle is long and tiring, something I'm not prepared for. You have made it clear what you want from this, and I would like to see a mutually beneficial agreement to avoid going into a courtroom.*"

She smirked as she finished reading her perfectly curated letter.

"Jackson, could you come take a look at this?" she called out, her tone steady but inside, her thoughts churned with anticipation.

The sound of boots scuffing against hardwood preceded Jackson's arrival. He leaned against the door frame, his short, messy hair giving him a perpetually untousled look that was both endearing and maddeningly attractive.

"Sure thing, April." His light eyes scanned the page, eyebrows knitting together as he processed her words. "It reads like you're laying down arms, giving up."

"Exactly." April tapped the paper with a slender finger, a wry smile playing on her lips. "It's part of the strategy, Jackson. In law, there's a dance between the lines—a psychological game."

He tilted his head, regarding her with a mix of confusion and newfound respect. "You want them to think you're backing down?"

"Let their guard down, more like," she corrected softly, her gaze meeting his. "On paper, I'm the weary ex-lawyer, beaten down by the system. But when we meet face to face..." A spark of cunning lit up her eyes, and for a moment, the calculated lawyer from her past life shone through.

Jackson chuckled, a low rumble that seemed to fill the space between them. "And then you strike."

"Exactly," April affirmed, refolding the letter with meticulous care. Her mind raced with the countless repercussions, the delicate balance of risk and reward. The faint scent of pine from the Christmas tree in the corner wafted over, a poignant reminder of the season's joy that she'd temporarily set aside.

"April, you sure about this? It's pretty bold to assume that they'll think you're giving in," Jackson said, his voice laced with concern yet edged with admiration.

"Bold has served me well in the past," she replied, her confidence unwavering. Yet beneath the surface, a flutter of uncertainty reminded her of the stakes at play. This was more than just a building; it was her chance at a fresh start, at weaving the strands of her life back together in this small town.

"Then I'm behind you all the way." Jackson's affirmation was simple, yet it bolstered her resolve like a sturdy beam supporting the very structure of her future bed and breakfast.

"Thank you. That means more than you know." April tucked the letter into an envelope, sealing her gambit within its papery confines. Her heart drummed a nervous beat, but she allowed no tremor to seep into her hands. Everything hinged on the city's next move, and she had just made hers.

"Brilliant, April. Absolutely brilliant," Jackson's voice was tinged with both awe and a hint of worry as he leaned back in his chair, observing her with those light eyes that seemed to see right through to the heart of things. "I just hate that it's eating into your holiday. Christmas is only a week away."

April glanced again at the twinkling lights adorning the small fir tree in the corner of the room. The warm glow fought against the creeping shadows of the winter evening, a beacon of festivity she felt oddly detached from.

"Unfortunately, legal battles don't observe the calendar," she said, offering him a wry smile. "But don't worry. Once this is over, we'll have plenty of time for holiday cheer."

She hoped her words sounded more convincing than they felt. In truth, she longed for a respite, to immerse herself in the simple, comforting rituals of the season. But those dreams would have to wait; there were bigger fires to extinguish first.

"Alright then," Jackson acquiesced, though his brow furrowed slightly. "Just make sure you save some energy for celebrating."

With a nod, April picked up the envelope containing her calculated surrender—or rather, the illusion of one. She stood up, smoothing the creases of her shirt with hands that betrayed no sign of the turmoil churning within.

"I'm going to drop this in the mailbox," she declared, holding the envelope before her like a shield. "Wish me luck."

"Good luck, April," he said, but his gaze lingered on her a moment longer, revealing his unsaid thoughts—that perhaps she needed more than luck.

Pushing through the front door, the cold winter air slapped at her cheeks, the night's chill sinking into her bones. She strode confidently to the mailbox, an old friend painted a cheerful red, now marred by vandalism. It hung open, its mouth agape, a deep dent marring its side while ugly black paint splattered across its surface like the careless flicks of a disdainful brush. A sigh escaped her lips. Of course, even the mailbox wasn't immune to the town's undercurrents of discord.

"Seems fitting," she muttered under her breath. They'd tried to taint her efforts at every turn, why should her mailbox be spared?

Carefully, she slipped the envelope into the box, the click of the metal lid closing sounding unusually final in the silent night. She couldn't shake the feeling that this small act was more than just sending a letter—it was casting a stone into still waters, waiting for the ripples to reach distant shores.

With measured steps, she returned to the warmth of her home, the coldness of the outside world clinging to her like an unwelcome shadow. There was a heaviness to her movements, a reflection of the weight of the battles she faced.

Yet, she moved with determined grace, the faint hope that this strategy would be the turning point propelling her forward.

The moment April crossed the threshold, a rush of warmth enveloped her, chasing away the chill that had settled deep in her bones. She removed her coat with an exaggerated flourish, a dry chuckle rumbling from her chest.

"Jackson, you won't believe—" her voice dripped with irony, the words hanging mid-air as the shrill ring of the phone sliced through the cozy ambiance of the living room.

She halted, a hand frozen on the back of a chair, and cast a fleeting sidelong glance at Jackson. His eyes were fixed on her, reflecting the flicker of curiosity that danced in the air between them. With a swift motion, she plucked the phone from her pocket, the familiar weight of it pressing against her ear.

"April? It's Alice," came the voice, almost lost beneath the howling wind that seemed to claw at the other end of the line.

"Alice, what's—" Panic knotted in April's stomach as she gripped the phone tighter, a frown etching itself across her brow.

"Please, I need you here, now," Alice's plea cut through the static, urgent and raw. "Come to the house."

"Okay, I'll be right there," April said, her heart thundering against her ribs, a jolt of adrenaline sharpening her senses. She hung up and turned to face Jackson, her expression taut with concern. "We have to go, something's wrong at Alice's place."

Jackson was on his feet in an instant, his previous confusion replaced by a resolute determination that seemed to radiate from him like heat from a flame. "Let's go," he said, reaching for his jacket draped over the back of a kitchen chair.

As they hurried out of the house, the cold air bit at their faces, the festive lights strung along the eaves twinkling mockingly against the sky. April's mind raced with possibilities, each more unsettling than the last, as she followed Jackson's determined strides towards the truck.

"Whatever this is, we'll handle it together," Jackson said, his voice barely audible over the crunch of gravel underfoot.

April nodded, feeling a sliver of gratitude for his unwavering support. The world might be spinning out of control, but with Jackson by her side, she felt just a fraction more prepared to face whatever lay ahead.

CHAPTER SEVENTEEN

April's knuckles rapped against the weathered wood of Alice's front door, the sound oddly muffled by the sea breeze that wrapped around the small beach house. Moments passed before the door swung open, revealing Alice's worried face.

"I didn't know what else to do," Alice said, wringing her hands as she stepped aside to let April and Jackson in. Her voice carried the tremor of uncertainty that made April's heart clench with concern.

"What's going on? Show us," April replied, her instinct for conflict resolution kicking in despite her new, more tranquil life.

Alice nodded, leading them through the narrow hallway cluttered with coastal knick-knacks, each one whispering stories of sunny days and stormy nights. They emerged onto a wooden deck that overlooked the stretch of private beach, where the waves gently caressed the shore.

There, amidst the serenity, lay a discordant note—a horse, its chestnut coat dulled by distress, laying on the sand barely moving. April felt her breath catch at the sight, the animal's vulnerability striking a chord within her. She exchanged a glance with Jackson, his light eyes already reflecting a quiet determination.

"Doesn't look right," Alice murmured, gesturing helplessly toward the creature. "Hasn't really moved and won’t let me near it. I think it's sick or injured, must be bad for it to be all the way out here and not moving."

Jackson moved first, descending the wooden steps with a purposeful stride, his sturdy boots leaving deep impressions in the soft sand. April followed close behind, her own shoes feeling inadequate against the beach's vastness.

"Hey, girl," Jackson called softly as they approached the downed horse. They walked carefully, ensuring they wouldn't terrify the already nervous creature.

The mare's sides heaved with shallow breaths, her eyes showing whites as they flickered with fear. She needed them, that was for sure.

"Easy, we're here to help," April soothed, her voice steady despite the fluttering in her stomach. She had dealt with high-stakes situations in the courtroom, but this was different—more personal. She needed to help.

As they came closer, the horse shifted slightly, its hooves scuffing the sand, but it did not rise. Jackson crouched beside her head, offering a gentle hand, while April lingered at a respectful distance, her mind racing with worry.

"Look at her, April," Jackson said quietly. "Something isn't right."

April nodded, stepping closer to join him. She could see now the scrapes along the horse's legs, the way her breath seemed labored. The mare's eyes met April's, and in that gaze, she saw a silent plea for compassion that she could not ignore.

"Maybe she's sick," April said, sizing up the beast.

"Maybe," Jackson said, his voice low. He looked up at April, and for a moment their eyes locked—a shared mission binding them tighter than any words could express.

Together, they would save this lost soul, and perhaps, April thought, they were also saving pieces of themselves.

Jackson's hands moved with practiced ease, tracing the lines of the mare's form as he looked for clues to her distress. April observed his every move, her own heart pounding in time with the surf that gently caressed the shore. She could tell by the way his brow furrowed that he'd found something significant.

"April, come here," Jackson called softly, motioning her over with a nod.

She knelt beside him in the sand, the grains sticking to her palms. His hands guided hers, and together they carefully rolled the horse onto her side. The mare's belly was round and taut, unmistakably swollen with new life.

"Jackson, she's..." April began, her voice trailing off as realization dawned.

"Pregnant," he finished for her, "and not just a little. This girl is about to be a mama." He estimated with a gentle pat on the horse's side. "I'd say no more than a couple of weeks, probably less."

The news anchored April to the spot, her mind flooded with concern and amazement. A new life was on the horizon, and it was in their hands to usher it safely into the world. A sense of purpose swelled within her chest, stronger than any closing argument she'd ever delivered in the courtroom.

"Okay, we need to check for injuries. Carefully, now," Jackson instructed, already running his hands along the mare's legs, searching for wounds.

April followed suit, feeling the coarse hairs and the warmth of the mare's skin under her fingertips. The scrapes were superficial, thankfully, but the water and harsh sand had irritated them. As they worked, April spoke in hushed tones, words of comfort meant as much for the horse as for herself.

"Easy, girl. We've got you," she murmured, her hands steady despite the tremor of emotion in her heart.

"Let's see if we can get her standing," Jackson suggested. He positioned himself by the mare's shoulder, while April took her place by the haunches. They counted to three and then pushed gently but firmly against the horse's body.

It took several attempts, each one punctuated by soft grunts of effort and encouragement. The mare struggled at first, her instincts dulled by exhaustion, but slowly, as if trust was being built with every heave, she gathered the strength to rise.

"Come on, you can do it," April whispered, her tone laced with an urgency that belied her calm exterior.

Finally, with a monumental effort, the mare stood, wobbly but upright. April exhaled a breath she hadn't realized she'd been holding, relief flooding through her veins.

"Atta girl," Jackson praised, his eyes meeting April's. There was a glint of admiration there for both the horse and for April herself—a connection forged in the crucible of compassion.

They lingered for a moment, ensuring the mare's stability, before guiding her towards the path that led back to the ranch. With each step, April felt a bond forming between them and the animal in their care. It was as if the mare understood that these two humans would be her safe harbor in the storm of uncertainty that lay ahead.

In the quiet that enveloped them as they walked, April realized that this rescue might just be the beginning of something beautiful—not just for the mare, but perhaps for her and Jackson too.

To witness something as beautiful as the birth of a new foal, she would be honored.

April and Jackson led the mare away from the lulling waves. With each step, the sand gave way beneath their feet, a reminder of the urgency pressing upon them.

"Easy now," Jackson murmured, his voice a soothing balm against the mare's skittish nerves. He walked beside her, a steadying presence as they navigated the uneven terrain.

April couldn't help but admire his gentle manner with the animal. She knew that finding a trailer would take too much time—time this expectant mother didn't have. As they moved forward, the ranch came into view, a comforting silhouette against the twilight sky. Her heart lightened at the sight; they were almost there.

"Jackson, do you think she knows we're trying to help her?" April asked, her hand stroking the mare's neck as they walked. She could feel the rhythmic pulse of life beneath her fingers, a testament to the new one waiting to be born.

"Animals have a sense of these things, I believe," he replied, his eyes never leaving the mare. "She'll understand soon enough when she's safe and sound in the stall."

As they approached the barn, April's mind raced with what needed to be done. The list of tasks was long, but her spirit was undaunted. This was why she had left her old life behind—a chance to make a difference, to nurture and protect.

Inside the stall, the mare's breathing eased amidst the familiar scent of hay and wood. April fetched some apple slices, offering them up with a tender smile. "Here you go, girl," she cooed, delighting in the soft nuzzle against her palm.

"Good job," Jackson said, watching the mare accept the treat. His hands roamed over her coat, checking for anything amiss, his touch precise and knowledgeable. It was clear he had done this many times before.

"Jackson, how can we make sure she's comfortable until..." April let the question hang, knowing the answer was complex.

"We'll monitor her throughout the night. Keep her calm, make sure she stays hydrated, and has everything she needs," he explained, his gaze intense and focused. "You're doing great, April. She's in good hands with us."

A swell of pride filled April's chest. Here she was, a former lawyer, now knee-deep in sawdust and equine care, and yet she'd never felt more purposeful. "I just want her to be okay," she whispered, more to herself than to Jackson.

The mare shifted, a quiet snort escaping her as if in response to April's concern. In that moment, April felt a profound connection to the creature before her—a shared understanding that transcended species.

"Me too, April," Jackson agreed softly, his light eyes meeting hers. "We'll get her through this. Together."

In the dim light of the stall, as the world outside grew quiet, April allowed herself to imagine the possibilities that lay ahead. A ranch bustling with life, a bed and breakfast filled with guests, and maybe, just maybe, a chance at love again. But for now, her focus remained on the mare, on the precious life she carried, and on the nurturing sanctuary she had built within these walls.

"Rest now," she murmured, both to the mare and to her own restless heart. "We've got a big few days ahead of us."

CHAPTER EIGHTEEN

The barn doors were thrown wide open, allowing the warm light of the golden hour to flood in and bathe the scene in an ethereal glow. The other horses had already been fed and were sprinting around the pastures.

April stood in a comfortable silence, her dark hair catching the light as she gently brushed the pregnant mare. April's dedication had been relentless, spending long hours in the barn with the mare, monitoring every aspect of her care.

She had even read up on equine gestation and made sure to consult with Jackson on any potential concerns. Then she'd called a vet to ensure the horse would be checked out before the baby was born.

At first, the mare had been cautious. She was clearly thankful for the shelter, taking time in the warmer barn to rest and eat. But it took April four tries to get her to allow brushing.

April was determined to make it a part of their routine. And two days later, here she was, able to brush the mama without any problems.

"Hey Mom, how's it going?" Georgia asked, stepping into the barn and scaring her mother, who was in the moment.

"Oh, hi, honey. It's only been two days since she's come in, but she's improving a lot after being under our care," April explained, her voice tender and filled with affection. "She's due any day now, and we need to keep her as comfortable and happy as possible."

April noticed Georgia staring at them with love in her eyes. April realized that her daughter had probably never seen her so still, so at ease. She'd always been a busy lawyer, fighting and serious at work. And now, this was her work.

"Would you like to brush her?" April offered, sensing Georgia's desire to be closer to the mare. Georgia nodded eagerly, her wavy hair bouncing as she moved.

"Of course! I'd love to help," she replied, taking the brush from her mother and stroking the mare's side with gentle, rhythmic motions. The mare leaned into the touch, basking in the attention from both women.

"Want to feel the baby?" April asked, a soft smile playing on her lips. Georgia's eyes lit up, and she nodded vigorously.

"Absolutely," she whispered, placing her hand on the mama horse's belly. Together, they shared a sweet moment, lost in the wonder of new life stirring beneath their fingertips.

The gentle warmth of the barn's interior shielded them from the chilly winter air outside. The mare, her breath visible in the cool atmosphere, shifted slightly as they continued to brush her. April noticed the concern in Georgia's eyes as she looked at the pregnant animal.

"Is it going to be safe?" Georgia asked hesitantly, her green eyes searching her mother's face for reassurance.

"Of course," April said with a confident smile. "We have a vet specialist coming tomorrow to make sure everything is in order."

"On Christmas Eve?" Georgia questioned, raising an eyebrow.

April nodded. "It's a special circumstance. Besides, I'd give anything to make sure this poor horse is ready to give birth and that she's comfortable." Her thoughts lingered on the responsibility they had taken on, but the connection they'd already formed with the mare made every effort worthwhile.

As they finished brushing the horse, the soft swishing sound of the brush against her coat filling the space, April decided to broach a subject that had been on her mind. "So, what are you up to tonight?"

"Going out with friends," Georgia replied without elaborating further, her gaze focused on the mare.

April bit her lip, curiosity piqued by her daughter's secrecy. She hadn't met these friends yet, and while she wanted to give Georgia the freedom to explore new relationships, she couldn't help but feel concerned.

It felt like Georgia was hiding something. She could never look April in the eye when she explained where she was going. Despite asking her about her outings often, Georgia was always vague in her answers.

"That sounds fun," April replied casually, trying not to pry. "I hope you have a great time."

"Thanks, Mom," Georgia smiled, her eyes meeting April's briefly before returning to the horse. "I will."

As they stood together in the warm, hay-scented air of the barn, April couldn't help but marvel at the bond they shared, as well as the one they were forming with the mare. Despite the uncertainty of their future and the questions that remained unanswered, the love and trust within their small family was unwavering. And in this moment, that was enough to keep the worries at bay.

"Anyway, I should get going, too," April said as she checked her watch. "I still have some last-minute Christmas shopping to do." She sighed, feeling the pressure of time weighing on her. It had been a busy few days, and she hadn't had a chance to focus on the upcoming holiday.

"Okay, Mom," Georgia said, giving her a smile. "Don't worry about us. We'll be just fine."

"Alright, sweetheart," April replied, gently patting the mare's side before leaving the barn. As she walked towards the house, she shook off the hay clinging to her clothing and considered what gifts might bring a smile to her daughter's face.

Once inside, April quickly washed up, changed into a cozy sweater and jeans, and grabbed her purse before heading out for a day of shopping in town.

As April drove down the gravel driveway, she noticed something amiss along the property line. Her eyes narrowed as she spotted a section of the new fence that Jackson had been working on. The wooden slats were broken, with some pulled out of the ground and metal stakes twisted at a ninety-degree angle. It was clear that no animal could have caused such damage.

It was more vandalism. Her heart sank. She gripped the steering wheel and took a deep breath. It was hard to keep her anger under the surface.

This wasn't the first time their property had been targeted, but it was the most brazen act yet. She wondered why they couldn't simply leave her alone.

April tried to refocus her thoughts on the task at hand – finding perfect gifts for her loved ones. Yet, as she continued down the driveway, her mind kept wandering back to the damaged fence.

Perhaps it was finally time to invest in security cameras, she thought. They couldn't afford to keep repairing the damages, and more importantly, she needed to ensure the safety of her family and their animals.

"Cameras," she whispered to herself, committing to the idea. "That'll help."

Resolute in her decision, April turned onto the main road and headed towards town, her heart a mix of holiday anticipation and worry over the troubles lurking just beyond the safety of their home.

But for now, she would focus on the warmth of the season, knowing that together, they would face whatever challenges came their way.

CHAPTER NINETEEN

April strolled through the aisles of the quaint general store, her dark hair tucked neatly behind her ears. The store's antique wooden shelves were filled with an assortment of trinkets and treasures, each one catching her eye as she searched for the perfect Christmas gifts.

She admired a delicate porcelain teacup, its intricate floral pattern reminiscent of the ones her mother used to collect. With a satisfied smile, she added it to her basket, confident that Georgia would appreciate its beauty.

Next on her list was her secret Santa gift. Her eyes scanned the shelves for something unique and thoughtful. The ladies would appreciate anything she gave them, but she wanted to be sure it was special.

She picked up a set of hand-carved wooden spoons, considering their quality and weight. The third spoon had a lovely design with a horse and a chicken. And that's when it hit her.

She suddenly realized there was someone else she'd completely forgotten about. Her heart leaped at the thought of his name: Jackson.

"Jackson" was written on the list in her neat cursive, but somehow, her mind had skipped over it in the whirlwind of gift-hunting. She remembered the knife she'd picked out weeks before, with a beautiful horse engraving on the handle. It seemed fitting for Jackson, with his "mysterious ranch hand"-vibe. But now that their relationship had deepened, she wondered if it was enough.

He had been nothing but kind and helpful since the day she arrived at the ranch. And as they spent more time together, April felt a strong connection to him.

But now that their relationship had deepened, she wondered what kind of gift she could get him to show that she truly cared as much as she did.

April nodded thoughtfully, her mind racing as she tried to come up with the perfect gift idea. She knew she had been scatterbrained lately, juggling her newfound love life with the ranch and new horses, the bed and breakfast. The pressure to find the perfect gift for Jackson only added to her stress.

As April continued her search, she couldn't shake the feeling that the knife alone wouldn't be enough to show Jackson how much he meant to her. It was a beautiful piece, but it lacked the personal touch she desired. Lost in thought, she barely noticed the store owner's final words before disappearing behind the counter.

She knew it wasn't always the gift itself, but the thought behind it. Still, she felt guilty that her gifts this year had been rushed and forgotten.

Taking a deep breath, April decided to leave the general store and explore other options for Jackson's gift. She recalled the outdoors shop down the road that always seemed to have unique items on display. Perhaps they would have something more suited to Jackson's interests, something he could actually use and enjoy.

She didn't want to get him something for work, but it was one of his biggest hobbies. Otherwise, she wasn't sure what else to get him.

The crisp winter air greeted her as she made her way down the cobblestone street, her boots crunching softly in the snow. The scent of pine filled her senses, reminding her of how much she loved this time of year. It was a season of love, warmth, and giving – all things she wanted to share with those she cared about most.

As she approached the corner, April glanced across the street and was surprised to see Georgia standing next to the town's massive Christmas tree.

Her daughter's wavy hair cascaded over her shoulders, contrasting beautifully against the twinkling lights. She was wearing the same clothes she wore just an hour ago when she stood in the barn beside April.

But it wasn't just the sight of Georgia that caught April's attention – it was the man whose arm was linked around hers.

"Isn't that...?" April murmured to herself, squinting to get a better look. It was unmistakably Alex, the boy Georgia had been seeing during Thanksgiving break.

"Focus, April," she muttered under her breath, trying to push the surprise from her mind. She couldn't afford to be sidetracked now; she still had gifts to buy, including one for the very person occupying her thoughts at this moment.

As she continued towards the outdoorsy shop, her mind churned with questions. What were Georgia and Alex doing together? Was their relationship more serious than April had initially thought? She couldn't help but feel a pang of guilt for not being more involved in her daughter's life lately.

She'd tried to be, but her daughter had been so distant lately. Georgia wouldn't answer any of her questions about where she was going and what she was doing. April worried about the lack of responses, but she never thought it would have been for the same reason as it was before. Alex.

April stood rooted in place, her mind churning as she watched Georgia and Alex from across the street. They seemed so at ease with one another, their laughter filling the air as they gazed at the twinkling Christmas tree. April's heart raced; it was evident that this wasn't just a casual fling.

The way they couldn't keep their hands off each other and the way their gazes lingered told the story loud and clear - this was no mere fleeting encounter. Georgia's hand delicately slid across Alex's chest. They laughed harder than she'd seen her daughter laugh in months.

"Mom, I promise you, it's nothing serious," echoed Georgia's voice in her head, recalling their conversation after Thanksgiving break. But the scene before her painted a different picture altogether.

"Hey, watch it!" A passerby jostled April out of her reverie, forcing her to take a step back. She shook her head, trying to refocus on her mission – finding the perfect gift for Jackson.

"April, get a grip," she muttered under her breath, turning away from her daughter's unexpected date and continuing toward the outdoorsy store. Her thoughts, however, stubbornly refused to leave Georgia and Alex behind.

A memory washed over her: it was just a few weeks ago when she had followed Georgia around town, her worry gnawing at her insides like an overzealous beaver. She remembered how Georgia had lied about being out with friends, only to discover her cozied up with Alex at a local café.

"Mom, why can't you trust me?" Georgia's hurt expression from that day haunted April. Now, as she saw them together again, she wondered if she had been too harsh on her daughter.

"Can I help you find something?" The shopkeeper's voice interrupted April's thoughts, drawing her attention to the rows of outdoor gear surrounding her.

"Uh, yeah," April stammered, trying to collect herself. "I need a gift for my boyfriend. Something practical but personal."

"Let me show you our custom-made items," the shopkeeper suggested, leading her toward a display of handcrafted goods.

As they walked, April couldn't help but think about her own journey to find love again. She had managed to move on after her divorce, embracing the possibility of a new relationship. Maybe it was time to extend that same grace to Georgia and trust her daughter's choices.

"Here's our selection of personalized items," the shopkeeper announced, gesturing to the display. "I'm sure you'll find something perfect for your boyfriend."

"Thank you," April said with a smile, hoping that she could also find a way to mend her relationship with Georgia as easily as selecting a gift from the shelf.

She picked something out before stepping out into the street yet again. April scanned the area for her daughter and her date. She saw them again, sitting down at a table drinking cocoa or coffee, she couldn't quite tell.

She just wanted her daughter to be safe. Thinking back to the last time she found out about this relationship, she knew she didn't handle it all that well. She'd yelled and panicked, wanting Georgia to be safer about it all.

Her reaction had been less than ideal—she had let her protective instincts take over, causing an ugly confrontation between them. No wonder Georgia didn't confide in her anymore. And with her own romantic life awakening after her divorce, April could understand why her daughter might want some privacy.

She knew Georgia deserved some time to herself. It didn't make it hurt any less that she didn't know what was going on in her daughter's life.

She shook her head at herself, chuckling ruefully. She was a hypocrite. Exploring her own love life while asking Georgia to disclose everything about hers, keeping it out in the open when she'd reacted poorly the first time.

It was time for both of them to spread their wings and explore new relationships, trusting that they would always have each other's backs no matter what challenges life threw their way.

CHAPTER TWENTY

April took a deep breath as she stepped into the settlement meeting room, her heart pounding in her chest. The room was small and stuffy, with a single window casting a beam of sunlight onto the polished oak table that dominated the space. Despite her nerves, determination burned within her like a steady flame.

Across from her sat Isaac, the wealthy local mayoral candidate, his smug expression sending a wave of irritation through April. His dark eyes seemed to gleam with confidence, as if victory was already assured. He leaned back in his chair, crossing one leg over the other, a barely restrained smirk on his face.

"Ms. April," he said, inclining his head slightly, "So glad you could make it."

"Isaac," April replied tersely, ignoring the condescending tone in his voice. She took a seat opposite him, adjusting her neatly pressed blouse and smoothing her hair behind her ear.

"Let's get started, shall we?" Isaac suggested, waving a hand toward the two lawyers who represented the town. They were an older man and a younger woman, both wearing crisp suits that spoke of authority and professionalism.

"Of course," the older lawyer began, a serious look on his lined face as he opened a folder and pulled out several documents. "As you know, Ms. April, the town has issued a cease-and-desist order regarding the wild horses on your property." He paused, glancing at April to gauge her reaction, but her face remained impassive.

"Alright," she said, folding her hands on the table. "What does that mean?"

April knew exactly what it meant. But she wasn't about to act like she was knowledgable in front of these people.

"The town feels that the presence of these animals is a clear danger to our community," the younger lawyer chimed in, her voice firm and resolute. "We understand that you have a fondness for them, Ms. April, but we must insist that they be removed from your property to ensure the safety of our citizens."

April's eyes narrowed slightly, and she feigned fighting to keep her voice steady as she responded. "I see," she said, her mind racing with thoughts of the pregnant mare and the other horses that had found refuge on her land.

She would do everything she could to keep them safe. She needed to, because no one else would. Her ranch was the only place on the island safe for them now.

It was Isaac's doing that the lawyers were here talking about this. It was supposed to be over when she filed for federal reserve protection. But it seemed he would never let it go.

She remembered their previous encounters, his efforts to undermine her plans for the ranch. It was clear that he wouldn't stop until he saw her defeated, but she refused to let him win.

"Furthermore," the older lawyer continued, "we are prepared to reimburse you for any costs incurred in moving the horses, provided that you agree to comply with our terms." He gestured to the documents in front of him, a pen poised in his hand.

"Ms. April," the younger lawyer added, her expression softening slightly, "we hope you understand that this is not a personal attack. We are simply trying to protect our town and its inhabitants."

"Of course," April replied, her face betraying nothing of the rage that simmered in her chest. "I appreciate your concern."

April stared at the documents as the lawyers continued their explanations, her dark eyes steady and focused. Internally, she braced herself, knowing that the moment to reveal her hand was fast approaching. Yet, she maintained a calm exterior, not giving them any indication of the confidence bubbling within her.

The faint scent of Isaac's cologne wafted in her direction, momentarily distracting her from the conversation. She shifted her gaze towards him, observing his self-assured smirk, and felt her determination harden further.

"Ms. April, do you understand why we're taking these measures?" the older lawyer asked, bringing her attention back to the matter at hand.

"Of course," April replied softly, playing her part as she pretended to be cowed by their arguments. Her heart pounded in her chest, but she kept her expression neutral.

If this was going to work, she needed to trick them into thinking that she was really giving up. Which she knew she would never do. In fact, she wondered why Isaac, after all of the fighting they'd been through, thought that she was going to give in this easily.

The image of the pregnant mare filled her mind, its gentle eyes gazing up at her as if seeking reassurance. The other wild horses seemed to gather around her in her thoughts, each one a symbol of the life she was determined to build on the island. Their very existence depended on her ability to protect them from Isaac and his machinations. The reason why she fought as hard as she did.

"Good," the younger lawyer said, relief evident in her voice. "We just want what's best for the town."

"Indeed," April murmured, her fingers curling around the edge of the table as she forced herself to remain silent and attentive. She knew that her moment would come soon enough, and when it did, she refused to let Isaac or anyone else stand in her way.

"Are there any questions you have for us, Ms. April?" the older lawyer inquired, leaning forward slightly.

"No," she responded, her voice barely above a whisper. She looked down at the documents once more, steeling herself for the inevitable confrontation. And as the lawyers waited for her response, April realized that her silence would only serve to make her eventual stand all the more powerful.

The older lawyer pushed his glasses up the bridge of his nose, shuffling a stack of papers before him. He picked up one document and held it out to April with an air of finality. "Ms. April, we understand that relocating the horses may be a burden. And you've told us that you want to settle out of court and come up with a solution that benefits us all. Therefore, we believe that this reimbursement will be the best option for us all."

"Please review the terms of this settlement agreement and let us know if they seem appropriate," the younger lawyer added, sliding another document across the polished mahogany table.

April's fingers trembled as she picked up the paper, her eyes scanning its contents. Her heart raced, but she knew that the time had come to fight back. Slowly, she raised her gaze from the document, her expression shifting from defeat to defiance.

"No, I don't think so," she said firmly, locking eyes with Isaac, who sat across from her with a smug grin that began to falter at her words.

The room fell silent, the atmosphere growing tense as everyone processed her response. The lawyers exchanged uneasy glances, while Isaac's face turned a shade darker, his narrowed eyes boring into her.

Just then, the doors to the meeting room swung open with a resounding thud, drawing all attention to the entrance. A tall woman in a smart business suit confidently strode into the room, her high heels clicking against the marble floor.

Her long, blonde hair was pulled back into a neat ponytail, and her blue eyes sparkled with determination. It was April's friend from the city, an expert in environmental law.

"Apologies for my tardiness," she announced, not sparing a glance at the stunned faces around the table. "Traffic was a nightmare."

"Amelia," April breathed, unable to conceal the smirk that tugged at the corners of her lips. Amelia nodded in response, her own expression one of cool confidence.

"Ah, Ms. April," Amelia said, taking a seat beside her friend. "I see you've been holding down the fort in my absence. Shall we proceed?"

The room remained silent, the lawyers and Isaac exchanging wary looks as they tried to make sense of this unexpected turn of events.

But in that moment, April felt a surge of hope course through her veins. With Amelia by her side, she was ready to face whatever challenges lay ahead – and protect the wild horses she had come to love.

"Are we ready to continue?" Amelia repeated, her voice firm and authoritative. She glanced briefly around the room, taking in the anxiety rippling across Isaac's smug facade and the sudden apprehension of the island's lawyers. Then she opened her briefcase and pulled out a thick folder filled with documents and photographs.

"Allow me to enlighten you on why this cease-and-desist order is not only unnecessary but also entirely unlawful," Amelia began, her voice cool and precise. "Firstly, the wild horses that reside on Ms. April's property are protected under several environmental laws and regulations. Removing them would not only be illegal but would also have dire consequences for the island's ecosystem."

April watched as Amelia expertly flipped through the folder, providing detailed information about the essential role the horses played in maintaining the local environment. Her heart swelled with pride and gratitude for her friend, who had so willingly come to her aid.

"Furthermore," Amelia continued, "since you all don't want to listen to reason, should my firm choose to prioritize this case, I assure you it will not bode well for the town or its reputation. My entire firm will be ready to dig into this town, uncovering everything about every single one of you. In fact, not dropping this case could result in significant financial and legal ramifications."

The room seemed to hold its breath as Amelia's words hung heavy in the air. The island's lawyers shifted uncomfortably in their seats, exchanging nervous glances. Isaac's face contorted into a mixture of disbelief and anger, his confidence clearly shaken.

"Given these circumstances, I strongly urge you to reconsider your position and drop this lawsuit immediately," Amelia concluded, closing her folder with a decisive snap.

The silence stretched on for a moment longer before one of the lawyers cleared his throat, his voice wavering slightly. "Very well, Ms. Amelia. We'll...we'll drop the case."

A triumphant smile spread across April's face as she locked eyes with Isaac, whose expression was now one of barely contained fury. He had underestimated her, just as she had hoped. But now, she had won – not only for herself but for the wild horses who called her land home.

Without a word, April stood up, her smirk still firmly in place, and confidently strode out of the meeting room. The sound of Isaac's protests and the lawyers' attempts to calm him down faded into the background as she walked away, her heart swelling with victory.

As she stepped outside, the sunlight warmed her face, and she couldn't help but smile even wider. She had made a difference today, protecting the wild horses and their precious habitat.

She knew there would likely be more attempts on the ranch. But now, she knew she could outsmart them.

CHAPTER TWENTY ONE

The flickering candlelight cast a warm glow over the dimly lit restaurant, reflecting off the polished wooden table. April nervously fiddled with her silverware, glancing around the cozy space of Giant's. Amelia, her closest confidante, sat across from her, looking relaxed and at ease.

"Amelia," April said softly, "I can't thank you enough for coming here to help me. You've always been there for me, and I truly appreciate your support. I really needed it."

"Of course, April," Amelia replied with a sincere smile. "You've helped me so much with my cases in the past; it's only fair that I return the favor. Besides, we're more than just colleagues, we're friends."

April felt a warmth spread through her chest at Amelia's words but couldn't shake the unease that plagued her. This restaurant belonged to her ex, Nigel, and despite her desire to avoid him, she found herself back in his territory. She glanced out the window, taking in the small town she had recently moved to, hoping to find solace in its quaint charm.

"Are you okay?" Amelia asked, concern evident in her voice.

"Yes, of course," she replied with a forced smile.

It wasn't her idea to come to Giant's. After all, April had asked where her friend wanted to go, because it was thanks to her that they'd won. Amelia wanted burgers, raving about the place she saw as she came into town. The only burger joint in Sandcrest was Giant's.

And so here she was, sitting in Nigel's restaurant, praying that he wouldn't see her. Hoping that she wouldn't have the same experience she had there with Jackson just a short few days prior.

April was going to suck it up and sit with her friend in the restaurant she picked out. What was the worst that could happen?

April took a deep breath, trying to focus on the here and now. Amelia was right – it was the best and only place for a burger in town.

And besides, she shouldn't let her previous relationship with Nigel overshadow the friendship and support she had found. Tonight, it was just two friends sharing a meal, not an ex-lover lurking in the shadows.

The comforting presence of Amelia by her side gave her the strength to face whatever lay ahead. And as the scent of sizzling burgers filled the air, April decided that maybe, just maybe, everything would be alright.

The door to the kitchen swung open, and out stepped a young waitress with a familiar face. Her eyes locked onto April's for a moment before she approached their table, the corners of her mouth curling into what seemed like a smirk. But then again, April thought, maybe it was just her imagination playing tricks on her.

"Here are your menus," Izzy said, placing them on the table with practiced ease. "My name is Izzy and I'll be your server tonight. I'll give you a few minutes to decide."

Her snide look made April roll her eyes. Of course, it was this woman who had to be their server. If she was able to spill a drink on April when she wasn't waiting her table, April couldn't imagine what she could do when she was the one getting their food. She wondered if she would be able to eat at all during this celebratory meal.

"Thank you," Amelia replied politely, while April simply nodded, trying her best to avoid making eye contact with the waitress.

As Izzy sauntered away, April sighed inwardly. Of all the people who could have been assigned to their table, why did it have to be her? She tried to shake off the nagging feeling that something wasn't quite right, reminding herself that everyone had told her she was probably overthinking things.

When Izzy returned to take their orders, Amelia began. "I'm definitely getting this Giant's burger."

"And how would you like that cooked?" Izzy asked as she jotted down in her notebook.

"Medium, please," she replied as she handed over her menu.

"I'll get the same. Medium rare with no tomato," April stated plainly, trying hard to push out a smile.

"Of course," Izzy replied, scribbling down their preferences. "I'll put these in right away." She collected their menus and disappeared back into the kitchen, leaving April and Amelia alone once more.

April let out a small sigh of relief, grateful for the temporary reprieve from Izzy's presence. As they waited for their food, Amelia steered the conversation towards the day's events.

"Can I just say you did an incredible job today," Amelia gushed, her eyes sparkling with admiration. "It would not have worked without you playing yourself down so much. You had them fooled."

"Thank you," April replied, a warm flush creeping up her cheeks. "But honestly, I couldn't have done it without your help and support. We make a great team."

"Agreed," Amelia said, raising her water glass in a mock toast. "To us."

"To us," April echoed, clinking her glass against Amelia's. And for a moment, everything felt right in the world – despite the unsettling presence of Izzy lurking just beyond their table.

Before long, the sound of approaching footsteps signaled the arrival of their food. Izzy reappeared with two plates in hand, a forced smile on her face as she set them down on the table. April couldn't help but feel that something was off but tried to brush it aside.

"Enjoy your meal," Izzy chimed before retreating once more.

April's eyes immediately zeroed in on the bright red slices of tomato peeking out from under the bun of her burger. A twinge of irritation flickered through her, but she hesitated to say anything. Amelia, on the other hand, cut into her burger and frowned at the charred interior, clearly not the medium she had requested.

"April, look at this," Amelia said, gesturing to her overcooked patty. "This isn't what I ordered."

April glanced at her friend's burger and then back at her own, realizing that ignoring the issue might not be an option after all. She bit her lip, reluctant to confront Izzy about their meals.

"Maybe we should say something?" Amelia suggested, already scanning the room for their waitress.

As if on cue, Izzy materialized beside their table, her expression far too smug for April's liking. It almost seemed as if she had been anticipating their complaints.

"Is there a problem with your burgers?" Izzy asked innocently.

"Actually, yes," Amelia replied, her voice firm but polite. "My burger was supposed to be cooked medium, and it's clearly well done. And April's has tomatoes when she specifically asked for none."

"Of course, no problem," Izzy said, though her tone implied otherwise. "I'll have these fixed for you right away."

"Thank you," April added quietly, forcing a smile. "We appreciate it."

With a nod, Izzy whisked their plates away, leaving April and Amelia in an uneasy silence. April felt a growing sense of unease, the nagging thought that perhaps Izzy's malice wasn't just a figment of her imagination.

"Am I imagining things, or does she really have it out for me?" April whispered to Amelia, her eyes following Izzy's retreating form.

"Let's just hope our burgers come back right this time," Amelia said, squeezing April's hand reassuringly.

As April's eyes followed Izzy, she caught sight of Nigel standing in the doorway to the kitchen. His arms were crossed, and his eyes locked onto the plates with a mixture of annoyance and disappointment. As Izzy approached him, he rolled his eyes dramatically before grabbing them from her hands and disappearing back into the kitchen.

April's heart clenched at the sight of her ex, and an unsettling thought wormed its way into her mind. Could it be Nigel who was working against her all along? Was he deliberately sabotaging their meal as some sort of twisted revenge?

"April? Are you alright?" Amelia's voice cut through her thoughts, bringing her back to the present moment.

"Uh, yeah, I'm fine," April replied, quickly looking away from the kitchen door. "Just thinking about...everything."

"Everything" was an understatement. Her failed marriage, her move back to this small town, her dreams of running a successful bed and breakfast – all of it seemed to be slipping through her fingers, bit by bit.

"You sure?" Amelia asked quietly. "It's just burgers. They'll bring us back new ones."

"Right, I know. Just really hungry," she joked, trying to lighten the mood.

She thought back to the day her and Nigel broke up. While it had been mostly mutual, Nigel had been visibly upset at the end of their relationship. He took his time after she admitted she thought they shouldn't be together.

He hadn't argued, but he also hadn't been happy to see her go. She knew they were both sad their relationship didn't work out. But she was the one initiating the breakup. She'd told him they weren't working, and he looked sad, melancholy.

What if he'd seen her with Jackson, her ranch hand, and jealousy had driven him over the edge? The vandalism and bad reviews plaguing her business seemed excessive for a simple breakup. But it wasn't entirely impossible that Nigel, in his fury, wanted to cause her pain by destroying what she cared about most.

As they waited for their corrected meal, April stole glances towards the kitchen, her mind racing with possibilities and suspicions. If Nigel truly was behind everything, she would have to confront him eventually

– not just for herself, but for the future of her business. And if Izzy was in on it too...

Well, she would deal with that when the time came. For now, all she could do was hope that her once-trusted friend hadn't turned into her worst enemy.

"April, hey," Amelia's voice pulled April back from her swirling thoughts, her eyes filled with concern. "Are you okay? You seem really lost in thought."

"Sorry, Amelia," April forced a smile, trying to anchor herself to the present moment. Her fingers tapped lightly on the worn wooden table, her gaze drifting over the cozy restaurant interior – the brick walls adorned with antique photographs, the soft glow of the vintage chandelier overhead. She couldn't help but feel a pang of nostalgia for the times she'd spent here before everything had gone awry.

"Talk to me," Amelia insisted gently, her eyes never leaving April's face. "What's going on in that head of yours?"

There was a part of April that longed to unload everything onto Amelia, to tell her about the suspicions growing in her mind like weeds. But she hesitated, knowing she couldn't risk making accusations without solid proof. And besides, Amelia had been through so much already. It wouldn't be fair to burden her further.

"Nothing," she lied smoothly, taking a slow sip of water to buy herself time. "Just thinking about all the work I still have ahead of me at the bed and breakfast."

"April," Amelia said softly, reaching across the table to place a hand over hers. "I know you're worried about your business, but you don't have to face this alone. Lean on me, okay?"

"Thanks, Amelia." April squeezed her friend's hand, touched by her unwavering support. "I promise, if I need help, I'll ask."

"Good," Amelia nodded, seemingly satisfied with her response. "Now, let's try to enjoy our meal once it gets here."

The two women fell into easy conversation, talking about lighter subjects – Amelia's latest cases, the quirky guests at April's B&B, and even the local gossip. It was a welcome distraction from the shadows lurking in the corners of April's mind.

Yet, as they laughed together over shared memories, April couldn't shake the feeling that she would have to confront Nigel and Izzy sooner rather than later. She needed answers – not just for her own peace of mind but for the sake of her new life in this small town.

"Amelia," April began, her voice softening with unspoken vulnerability. "I just want you to know how much I appreciate you being here. I don't know what I'd do without you."

"Hey," Amelia smiled warmly, her eyes shining with sincerity. "That's what friends are for, right?"

"Right," April agreed, returning her smile. But even as she allowed herself to be swept up in their conversation, she couldn't ignore the knowledge that a storm was brewing on the horizon. Someone was coming after her and her business.

And when the time finally arrived, she would face it head-on.

CHAPTER TWENTY TWO

April set her keys on the front desk of the bed and breakfast, her heart still warm from the conversation at Giant's. Though she was reluctant to eat the food out of fear of what Izzy might have done to their burgers.

Still, the conversation was nice. Getting to talk with her lawyer friend felt good. It was a familiar face that she needed in this busy time. It reminded her of why she came out here, what she was trying to accomplish.

A sense of satisfaction washed over her as she looked around the cozy lobby. It was the day before Christmas Eve, and all she wanted to do was bask in the festive atmosphere.

She noticed that there were more Christmas decorations than before – twinkling lights, vibrant wreaths, and delicate snowflakes adorned every corner. Her brows furrowed in thought as she wondered why the lights they'd taken down were now back up.

But she couldn't help, her eyes lighting up with joy. Every inch of the space seemed to be touched by the holiday spirit, making the bed and breakfast even more inviting.

Just then, Georgia emerged from the basement, her wavy long hair cascading over her shoulders. Her green eyes sparkled as she stepped into the transformed lobby, a satisfied smile playing on her lips.

"Mom, you like what I've done with the place?" Georgia asked, her voice full of hope and pride. "I felt like we could add a little more cheer closer to the holiday."

April's heart swelled with gratitude and admiration for her daughter's creativity. Aspiring to become an interior designer, Georgia had a knack for turning any room into a work of art while still maintaining its warmth and character. The lobby was no exception.

"Georgia, this is absolutely stunning!" April exclaimed, her eyes shining with happiness. "You've truly outdone yourself this time. How did you manage to make it even more beautiful than before?"

Her daughter's cheeks flushed with pleasure at the compliment. "Well, I figured since we're so close to Christmas, why not go all out?

Plus, I found some amazing decorations in the basement that I just couldn't resist using."

"Thank you, sweetheart," April said, her voice thick with emotion. "You've made this place feel like home again, and I couldn't be more grateful."

Georgia beamed, her heart swelling with love for her mother. Their bond had been rocky recently, but it was nice to see that Georgia still wanted to spend time with her and celebrate the holiday they both loved.

"Thank you, Georgia," April said, her hands gesturing to the adorned lobby. "This really is magical. You've captured the essence of a traditional Christmas perfectly."

"Of course, Mom!" Georgia replied, her green eyes sparkling with excitement. "After all, it's our first Christmas together in this beautiful house you've made a home."

As they continued admiring the festive decorations, the sound of a door creaking open interrupted their moment. The cranky guest from before, a middle-aged woman with pinched features, emerged from her room, glaring at the brilliant display.

"Really?" she huffed, planting her hands on her hips. "I thought I already complained about this. It's too bright! It's obnoxious. There's no need for anything this vibrant in here."

April's eyebrows knitted together as she stepped protectively in front of Georgia, shielding her from the guest's negativity. This was a special moment between them, and she wouldn't let anyone ruin it.

"Excuse me, but—" April began, but the woman cut her off.

"Look, I'm not here to celebrate the holidays," the woman snapped, her voice icy. "All these lights and cheesy decorations make it impossible to forget that it's Christmas time. Can't you tone it down a bit?"

Rolling her eyes, April tried to maintain her composure as the woman's complaints washed over her like a cold wave. The warmth of the twinkling lights contrasted sharply with the chill emanating from the irate guest. In the background, Georgia looked on, concern etched on her face.

"Are you quite finished?" April inquired, her tone firm yet polite. The disgruntled guest hesitated before nodding, her eyes still narrowed.

"Fine," she muttered, turning to leave. But April wasn't ready to let her go without making a point.

"Wait," she called out, capturing the woman's attention once more. "I just want to say that our family is going to celebrate the holiday spirit this year. These decorations and lights bring joy to us, and I believe they do the same for most of our guests."

The woman scoffed, but April pressed on. "If you have a problem with it, there's a Holiday Inn down the road. You're welcome to stay there and leave our little joyous B&B alone." Her voice had been calm but assertive, reminiscent of her days standing up in the courtroom.

In the moment, April felt good getting it off of her chest. She was standing up for her beliefs and this little home that had taken forever to get right. But deep down, she knew that it might come back to bite her. Still, she was sick of having to explain why she was excited and ready for the holiday.

The guest gasped, taken aback by April's unwavering stance. Without another word, she retreated to her room, leaving April and Georgia standing in the lobby.

"Mom, that was amazing!" Georgia exclaimed, her green eyes sparkling with admiration. April allowed herself a small smile, feeling emboldened by her daughter's praise.

"Thank you, sweetheart," she replied, glancing around at the beautiful decorations that her daughter had so lovingly arranged. "I couldn't let her ruin this for us."

Georgia's face fell slightly, and she sighed. "Actually, Mom, I do have to leave tonight. I promised a friend I'd help her with something."

"Really?" April's heart ached at the prospect of her daughter leaving once again, especially now that they were bonding over their shared love of Christmas. "Do you have to? We're so close to Christmas, and I'm so proud of what you've done here. I'd love to spend some time with you."

"Mom, I promise I'll be back, and we can hang out all Christmas long. I won't let anything get in the way of our time together," Georgia assured her, reaching for April's hand and giving it a gentle squeeze.

April sighed, knowing she couldn't keep her daughter from her responsibilities. "Alright, Georgia. Just promise me you'll drive safely and come back soon."

"Of course, Mom," Georgia replied, smiling as she hugged April tightly. "I love you."

"I love you too."

Reluctantly, April released her daughter from the embrace and watched as Georgia grabbed her coat. Her heart felt heavy with a mixture of pride and sadness at the thought of spending another evening alone in their festive bed and breakfast.

"Alright, I'll see you soon," April said, trying to hide the disappointment in her voice.

"Bye, Mom!" Georgia called out, grabbing her coat from the front desk.

Just before Georgia was able to open the door, it pushed open from the outside. April half expected it to be Kristy, the other half thought it might be Jackson stopping in from the farm.

"Uh, oh... Hi," came from the doorway. April's eyes widened as she saw the tall, handsome man with kind blue eyes and sandy brown hair closing the door behind him. His cheeks were flushed from the cold, and snowflakes clung to his coat.

"Alex!" Georgia gasped, taking a step back from the door. Her face was a mixture of surprise and terror, clearly unprepared for her mother's reaction to seeing him.

"Hey, Georgia," Alex said sheepishly, rubbing the back of his neck. "I... I'm just stopping by."

Georgia's eyes slowly crept over to her mother, who was waiting to hear the explanation. The silence threatened to choke them as they all waited for April's response to seeing the man she'd yelled at before Thanksgiving in her house again.

CHAPTER TWENTY THREE

An uncomfortable hush hung heavy in the sun-dappled living room of the Victorian house. The light that filtered through the lace curtains cast a dappled pattern over the three of them, creating an almost dreamlike scene that clashed with the tension. She stood there, her medium-length dark hair framing her face as she regarded the young man who had just crossed the threshold.

"Georgia," April began, her voice measured but carrying a layer of frost, "you said you were going to help a friend with something tonight."

Georgia, poised at the edge of the antique settee, her wavy long hair a curtain around her anxious green eyes, took a breath before speaking. "Mom, I can explain—"

"Was it a date with Alex what you actually had planned?" April cut her off, her gaze shifting to the boy, searching his face for something she hadn't seen before.

Alex shifted between his feet nervously. April was still trying to decipher what was going on between them. She didn't want to push or prod. But she wanted the truth. Was her daughter lying to her all this time, like she was when April saw them at the Christmas tree in town?

Georgia's hands fidgeted at the hem of her dress—a nervous tick April knew all too well. "Yes," she confessed, her words barely above a whisper. "I was going to go on a date with Alex tonight."

April processed this information, her mind racing but her exterior calm. She gave a slow nod, the disappointment clear in her eyes even as she worked to keep her emotions in check. A tight smile briefly crossed her lips, one honed from years of courtroom battles where personal feelings had no place.

"I see," April said with a controlled calmness. "That's disappointing, Georgia. Not just the lie, but that you felt you couldn't tell me."

Georgia looked down, a blush creeping over her fair skin. She was clearly nervous, but ready for the brunt of her punishment. Ready to be yelled at just as they were the last time this happened. The last time April found out, she was running around town with a strange boy.

"However," April continued, nervously considering her options, "how about we turn this evening around? Would you two like to have dinner with me here instead?"

Georgia's eyes widened in surprise, mirroring the shock that flickered across Alex's face. April caught a hint of relief in their expressions. It was a peace offering, an olive branch extended in the quiet battlefield of their home.

"Really, Mom?" Georgia's voice held a mixture of hope and wariness, as if expecting a trap. "You don't have to do that."

April nodded, already mentally cataloging what ingredients she had in the kitchen. "If you're seeing this man, then I'd like a chance to get to know him. If you'll give it to me."

Perhaps it was time to let the past settle and give this boy a chance to prove himself. If not for her own curiosity, then for the sake of her daughter's happiness. After all, Georgia was a creative soul, vibrant and fiercely independent. She deserved the chance to make her own choices, even if April had to learn to step back a little.

"Well, we already had plans," Georgia began explaining nervously. Her words rambling out of her mouth.

Just as April was about to let them leave, Alex chimed in. "No, we should stay and have dinner."

Georgia looked up at the man in surprise, then back at her mother. April could tell her daughter was still cautious about the invitation. Which made sense to her because of the history. But April wanted to make new history. Of being a mother who cared *and* let her daughter make her own decisions.

"If you're really sure," Georgia replied with a small smile.

"I'd really like that," April affirmed, her heart thawing just enough to accommodate this new plan, this small step towards understanding her daughter—and maybe, just maybe, opening herself up to the possibility of getting to know the boy, or at least coming to a truce.

Georgia and Alex exchanged a glance, their eyes a silent conversation within the confines of April's warmly lit living room. The flickering shadows from the overhead chandelier cast a hesitant dance across their faces as Georgia turned back to her mother.

"This sounds... really nice, actually," Alex said, his voice even but carrying an undertone of earnestness that had been absent before. "Thank you, April."

April felt a warmth blossom in her chest. She didn't deserve this openness, not after the way she had let suspicion color her judgment earlier. But here they were, ready to break bread together and perhaps mend a few fences along the way.

"Then it's settled. Let me get started on dinner," she said, turning towards the kitchen with a sense of purpose.

As she set about the task of preparing the meal, the sounds of muffled conversation drifted from the dining room. She couldn't quite catch the words, but the cadence was comfortable, laughter punctuating the dialogue now and then. April found herself smiling at the sound, a stark contrast to the silence that had blanketed the house moments ago.

She chopped vegetables methodically, the rhythmic slicing a soothing counterpoint to her roiling thoughts. If only she had approached this differently from the start, offered an open hand rather than a furrowed brow. Georgia was no longer a child to be guided at every turn; she was a young woman with a vision for life that was all her own.

April stirred the pot simmering on the stove, the aroma of herbs filling the kitchen. She allowed herself a moment to lean against the counter, her gaze lost in the steam rising from the bubbling sauce. It was time to trust Georgia's choices, to recognize the maturity in her decisions. And perhaps, this meal could be the first step in understanding the young man who had captured her daughter's heart.

"Everything smells amazing, Mom," Georgia called out, her words floating over the scent of garlic and thyme.

"Almost ready," April replied, her voice steadier than she felt.

With a deep breath, she turned back to her culinary efforts, determined to make this evening one of new beginnings. For her daughter's sake, and maybe, just a little, for her own.

April entered the dining room, the weight of the ceramic dish warming her palms as she set it down with a soft thud against the polished wood of the table.

She noticed how the golden light from the chandelier above cast a glow on the colorful medley of roasted vegetables and lemon-herb chicken she had prepared. The room fell into a respectful hush, punctuated only by the clink of serving spoons against the dishes as they all began to help themselves.

"Thank you for this meal, April," Alex said, his voice sincere, breaking the silence as he looked up from his plate with a smile that crinkled the corners of his eyes.

"Of course, Alex. It's my pleasure." April returned the smile, feeling the tension in her shoulders ease just a fraction. "Tell me about yourself," she encouraged, her tone gentler than before.

Alex nodded, a strand of his hair falling over his forehead as he leaned forward, eager to share. "Well, I'm currently studying to be an electrician at the local tech school. It's part-time, so I balance that with work at the bookstore downtown."

"Sounds like a full schedule," April commented, her fork pausing mid-air as she listened, picking up on the earnestness lacing his words.

"Yeah, it can be a bit much, but I manage," he replied, taking a bite of his food. "Plus, I help out my grandmother quite a bit. She's getting on in years and could use the extra hand around the house."

April chewed thoughtfully, watching him speak. His hands were rough, she noticed—workman's hands—yet they moved with care as he cut his food. There was a quiet strength about him, a diligence that seemed woven into the fabric of his being.

And he was kind. Understanding the importance of taking care of family, those who need us. His values were strong, comforting April with his large heart.

Her daughter had always been drawn to creativity, to those who could see beyond the mundane. In Alex's grounded nature and practical skills, April saw a complement to Georgia's vibrant imagination.

"Your grandmother must appreciate that," April said, finding herself genuinely curious about the layers of Alex's life.

"She does," Alex laughed softly, his face lighting up with fondness. "She taught me everything I know about fixing things. Says I've got a natural talent for it."

"And what about your plans after school?" April probed further, setting down her utensils to give Alex her full attention.

"I'd like to start my own electrical business someday. Maybe even specialize in eco-friendly solutions. You know, do my part for the environment and the community." His explanation was sprinkled with hope, a reflection of youthful ambition tempered by realistic goals.

April felt a smile tug at her lips, impressed by his vision. In this moment, seated at her table, sharing in the meal she had prepared with careful hands, she understood why Georgia saw something special in Alex.

He wasn't just a young man working towards a trade; he was someone with dreams that reached beyond himself, someone who cared deeply for family and the world around him.

"Georgia has a creative soul," April ventured gently, glancing at her daughter whose eyes shone with pride. "It seems to me you both could build something quite beautiful together."

"Thank you," Alex said, his voice soft with gratitude. "I think so too."

As the dinner progressed, April allowed the conversation to flow, weaving her way through Alex's responses, each one revealing more of the character beneath the surface.

With every answer, April's initial misgivings were slowly replaced by a burgeoning respect for the young man who was more than just a suitor for her daughter—he was a person of substance, kindness, and ambition. And perhaps, just maybe, he was exactly the type of person she hoped would find their way into Georgia's heart.

The last of the evening light filtered through the half-drawn curtains, casting a warm glow over the remnants of their meal. In the dining room's soft illumination, Georgia's green eyes sparkled with mischief as she began to recount the day that had led her steps—and her heart—to Alex.

"Mom, you should've seen Alex with this tiny squirrel," she said, a laugh bubbling up. "Right there in the middle of Main Street traffic, he was trying to be like a knight in shining armor."

Alex shifted modestly in his seat, his cheeks tinged with an embarrassed rose. "I just didn't want the little guy to get hurt. I didn't realize he was going to run into that store. Thankfully, no one else got hurt."

But April saw it in the tender tilt of his head, the careful way his hands folded on the table—this was the mark of true compassion. Her earlier anger seemed distant now, misplaced amidst the warmth that filled the dining room. She cleared her throat softly, releasing the tension that had been coiled within her.

"Alex, I owe you an apology." Her voice was sincere, tinged with regret. "I jumped to conclusions before without giving you a chance. That was wrong of me. I was blinded by my frustrations with not knowing what was going on."

Georgia's fork paused mid-air, and Alex's hand stilled. The air hummed with unspoken words as April continued, "I should've been more open-minded, asked questions first. It seems you're a much better fit for Georgia than I realized. I didn't understand it was like this. This... real."

"April, it's okay," Alex replied, his tone kind and forgiving. "We all get protective of the ones we love."

"Thank you, Alex." April felt a weight lift from her shoulders, her heart swelling with relief as the tight line of Georgia's mouth softened into a smile.

"Mom, no one's perfect. We just learn as we go, right?" Georgia reached out, placing her hand atop April's with a gentle squeeze.

"Right," April echoed, feeling the truth of those words resonate within her.

Laughter soon returned to the room, light and easy, as they shared stories and memories—April learning more about Alex, about his aspirations and the thoughtful ways he cared for his grandmother.

The evening unfolded like a well-loved book, each page revealing more depth to the characters she thought she knew. As Alex entertained them with tales of his tech school adventures and shared dreams of wiring homes so they could be safe and beautiful, April couldn’t help but see the parallels with her own journey of renovating her childhood house into something new.

When it came time for Alex to leave, his departure was marked by a chorus of goodbyes and promises to do it again soon. Georgia walked him to the door, their laughter a fading echo as April tidied up the table, stacking dishes and wiping down surfaces.

She peered through the window, watching the young couple share a quiet moment under the porch light. Their silhouettes were a testament to young love—hopeful, resilient, and bright against the backdrop of the small-town night.

As the door closed behind them, April leaned back against the counter, a contented sigh escaping her lips. She felt better knowing that she'd given Alex a fair chance.

Maybe next time, Georgia would come to her with the truth.

CHAPTER TWENTY FOUR

The chime of the grandfather clock in the foyer struck a warm, melodic tune, signaling the approach of dusk on Christmas Eve. April stood on the porch of her home, her breath visible in the crisp air as she waved goodbye to the last of her guests—the particularly cantankerous woman who hadn't appreciated her festive zeal.

"Happy holidays!" she called out with a forced cheerfulness, her voice laced with undisguised relief.

As the woman's car disappeared down the winding driveway, lined with snow-dusted pines, April let out a long sigh and turned back toward the grand Victorian house that had been both her childhood home and her latest passion project.

Twinkling fairy lights adorned the eaves, and wreaths of holly and ivy hugged the door frames. The sight brought a genuine smile to her face—one devoid of any obligation to please difficult patrons. She wrapped her arms around herself, holding onto the warmth of her victory over criticism.

"Finally, some peace," she murmured, her dark hair dancing in the chilly breeze as she admired the garlands twining up the porch's banisters.

The thought of tranquility was short-lived, however, as April remembered the one guest that needed her attention—the pregnant mare in the barn. With a sense of responsibility fueling her stride, she made her way across the frosted ground, her boots crunching with each step. The barn stood strong against the winter landscape, a silent sentinel guarding the equine family within.

"Easy girl," she whispered soothingly as she entered the stable. Her hand automatically went to stroke the mare's neck, feeling the coarse hairs under her palm. "Not long now."

April's nurturing words were abruptly cut off by the sharp gasp that escaped her lips. A splintered window frame caught her eye, the jagged edges of the wood sitting menacingly in the fading light. It had been cracked open, pierced through by, what looked like, something akin to a crowbar.

She rushed over, her heart pounding in her chest. The sinking realization that someone had tried to break into the barn set her blood boiling. Sure, they hadn't broken the glass, but if they had, even accidentally, it could have hit one of the horses.

Who could do this? On Christmas Eve, no less? The question hung in the frigid air, mingling with the soft nickers of the horses.

April examined the damage more closely, her lawyer-trained eyes searching for clues amidst the chaos. It wasn't just an act of mindless vandalism—it felt targeted, malicious even.

She clenched her fists, the protective instinct that had once fueled her courtroom battles now directed at her new life and the creatures depending on her.

"Ugh!" she said under her breath, her voice laced with fury. This wasn't just about property damage. It was about safety—the horses' safety.

An image of the mare, heavy with foal and vulnerable, flashed in her mind, and it stoked the fire of her anger further. Whoever was responsible had crossed a line, and April knew she couldn't let this pass. Not this time. The peace of her Christmas Eve had been shattered, but her resolve had crystallized into a fierce determination.

"Alright, enough is enough," she declared to the silent barn, her tone resolute. "We'll get to the bottom of this."

With the urgency of the situation propelling her forward, April secured the barn as best as she could, promising herself she'd take extra precautions from now on. Whoever was behind this would not intimidate her. This was her home, her sanctuary, and she would defend it with every ounce of her being.

The crisp evening air nipped at April's cheeks as she stormed out of the barn, her breath forming little clouds of steam that dissolved into the frosty Christmas Eve.

She marched with purpose to her car, the gravel crunching under her determined steps, a stark contrast to the jingle of festive decorations that swayed gently in the winter breeze.

Her medium-length hair was pulled back in a no-nonsense ponytail, and her fists were balled up in the pockets of her coat, each step towards the driver's door fueling her ire.

"Enough is enough," she muttered to herself, sliding behind the wheel. The ignition flared to life, the engine's growl mirroring the rage boiling within her.

As she drove down the winding road toward town, the twinkling lights of holiday cheer that adorned the streetlamps felt like a mockery of the turmoil inside her.

How could Nigel do this? After all, they had history—a shared past that should have bred respect, not this... sabotage.

April's knuckles turned white on the steering wheel. It wasn't just about the broken window; it was a direct assault on the sanctuary she'd built for herself and her animals after leaving the cutthroat world of law. They depended on her, trusted her, and she would not let them down.

The drive was short, but with each passing road, her thoughts raced faster. She wasn't prepared for a confrontation—she preferred evidence, hard facts, something her former career had ingrained deep within her psyche. But seeing her barn, her refuge, violated... it was personal now.

As she pulled up to Nigel's house, the quaintness of the snow-dusted roof and the wreath on the door did little to quell the fire in her chest. He'd be there, she knew. His restaurant, Giant's, was closed for the holidays. No escape, no excuses.

She didn't bother composing herself or rehearsing what to say. The moment Nigel's face appeared in the doorway, the words erupted from her like a geyser.

"Ridiculous!" she spat, her voice sharp as icicles. "Absolutely ridiculous, Nigel! Coming after me, my ranch, my horses? What were you thinking?"

"April, I—" Nigel began, but she cut him off with a dismissive wave.

"Save it! I've worked too hard for someone to come along and try to destroy it on a whim. I wouldn't have thought you to be a man of vandalism and petty attacks." The accusation hung heavy in the chilled air between them. Her heart pounded in her ears, a symphony of anger and betrayal.

"Look at me, Nigel. Look at what you're doing to me." Her eyes, usually warm and inviting, now bore into him with the intensity of her former courtroom glares. "I need to protect what's mine. And I won't let anyone—especially not you—threaten that."

In the moment, standing on his doorstep, the cold seeping through her boots and into her bones, April felt the full weight of her new life pressing down upon her. This wasn't just about mending fences or soothing bruised egos. This was about survival, about fighting for the dream she'd built from the ashes of her old life.

"Why are you doing this?" she demanded, her voice steady despite the tremble that threatened to betray her inner turmoil.

Nigel stood before her, and for a moment, the world held its breath, waiting for his reply.

Nigel's eyes widened, a flicker of genuine perplexity playing across his features. His mouth opened and closed, fish-like, as if words had abandoned him in the chilly evening air.

He stepped aside, a silent invitation into the warmth of his home. "April, I honestly don't know what you're talking about," he said, his voice laced with an earnest confusion that made April falter for just a heartbeat.

"Come in before you catch your death out here." Nigel's concern seemed so at odds with the vandalism at her ranch, with the poison penned on the internet that it gnawed at the edges of her anger.

Reluctantly, April crossed the threshold, her boots leaving faint prints on the welcome mat. The house smelled of cinnamon and something savory—evidence of Nigel's culinary prowess even on a day off. She wrapped her arms around herself, more out of a need to hold herself together than from the cold.

"Someone has been tearing apart my property," she started, the words tumbling out like the turmoil within her. "And they've been writing awful, untrue things online about the bed and breakfast."

"April, look at me," Nigel implored, stepping closer, his hands raised in a gesture of peace. "I haven’t done anything to hurt you or your place."

His brow creased with worry, and for a moment, she could see the man she once thought she knew—the man who'd shared dreams with her over late-night dishes of homemade pasta.

"Confused and hurt after our breakup, sure. But this?" He shook his head, strands of his dark hair falling across his forehead. "I saw you with Jackson, and yeah, it stung. But I care about you. I’d never go after what you love. Not now, not ever."

His words hung there, suspended in the air that now seemed too thick to breathe. Her heart pounded fiercely, a drumbeat of indecision.

For the first time, she wondered if he could be innocent. The Nigel she remembered struggled with expressing himself, often retreating behind the safety of his kitchen rather than confronting issues head-on. It wasn't like him to take such aggressive action.

"Then who would do this?" April whispered, though she hadn't meant to speak aloud. A whisper of vulnerability betrayed her usual fortitude as she turned away, staring out the window at the snow gently falling outside, each flake unique and transient, like the moments leading her here.

"I'm really sorry all of that is happening to you, but I promise I didn't do it," Nigel repeated.

She tried to think things through again, see them from a different perspective. But her brain was fogged with the anger, the weight on her shoulders that didn't seem to go away.

She looked Nigel up and down, recognizing that his expression held confusion and authenticity. "I'm going to get to the end of this. I'll find out what happened. And if it was you, I'll be very upset," she said before walking out the door.

April wasn't sure what to believe anymore. Nigel looked innocent, but she couldn't forget when he rolled his eyes at her food in Giant's. And she couldn't let go of the fact that no one else made sense.

No one knew her well enough to hit where it hurt, the bed and breakfast and now the ranch.

Isaac was the only one who truly hated her in town. And he always hit her in the legal sense. He wanted to take her down intellectually, mentally taking her past her limit. He wouldn't subject himself to something like vandalism.

She thought about her options as she drove home. All she knew for sure was that cameras would have to be installed. Then and only then could she be sure she would find out who did this.

CHAPTER TWENTY FIVE

April's fingers swiped across the glossy screen of her phone, a medley of camera models and security options dancing before her eyes. Her mind was a whirlwind of lenses and motion detectors as she considered the best way to protect her future bed and breakfast.

The soft chime of an incoming video call sliced through her concentration like a warm knife through butter. She glanced at the caller ID—Carl—and felt an involuntary smile tug at the corners of her mouth.

"Georgia, honey, come over here! Your dad's calling," April called out, her voice echoing slightly in the spacious lobby that still held echoes of its former grandeur. The space was a canvas waiting for a transformation, much like her life.

Georgia, with her cascade of wavy hair and those striking green eyes so like her father's, breezed into the room, a vision of youthful creativity. "Hey, Dad!" she beamed, leaning into the frame beside her mother.

"Hello, you two," came Carl's voice, crackly but warm over the phone. April tapped the screen, and suddenly his face filled their view, except it was almost unrecognizable under layers of theatrical makeup designed to transform him into something out of Alpine folklore.

"Carl, is that you under all that... artistry?" April chuckled, the sheer absurdity of his appearance making her heart feel light for the first time in days.

"Indeed, it is I," he declared with a playful flourish. "I'm about to join the Krampus festival here in Salzburg. You know how these things go." His grin was infectious, even beneath the faux menace of his costume.

Georgia laughed, a clear, bright sound that bounced off the walls. "Wow, Dad, you always did have a flair for the dramatic. That's some serious dedication."

"Ah, this? This is nothing compared to the Running of the Bulls last year," Carl said, his eyes twinkling merrily. "Or that time I joined the mime troupe in Paris."

"Always chasing the next adventure," April mused silently, her heart swelling with a blend of fond exasperation and respect. Here was a man who embraced life with both hands, never hesitating to leap into the unknown.

"Looks like you're ready to scare half of Germany," April teased, the words laced with affection. It was hard not to admire Carl's zest for life, even if it was one of the very things that had nudged them onto different paths.

"Only half?" Carl feigned disappointment, then winked. "I must be losing my touch."

"Never," April replied, her laughter mingling with Georgia's as they shared this moment, a snapshot of the new normal they were all navigating. It was strange, yet comforting, to find humor and warmth in the remnants of what used to be.

The frost on the windows glinted as if trying to match the twinkle in Carl's eyes, a tiny constellation of light that danced across his face on April's phone screen.

"Merry Christmas, you two," he said, his voice bubbling with the same exuberance that had him donning the Krampus makeup. "Just wanted to make sure my favorite ladies knew they were on my mind today."

"Of course, we are," Georgia replied, her tone playful yet sincere. April watched her daughter, the ease with which she interacted with Carl, and felt a warmth unfurl within her chest—a stark contrast to the chill seeping through the glass.

"Seems like you're having quite the adventure over there," April chimed in, her voice steady despite the swell of mixed emotions. She glanced at the calendar hanging beside the door, its festive scenes a reminder of the season's joy.

"Life's one big festival, right?" Carl laughed, the sound rich and hearty. "Got to enjoy the show while it lasts."

April's lips quirked into a half-smile, recognizing the truth in his words. As she ran a hand through her dark hair, a habit from her lawyering days when she needed to gather her thoughts, she felt the final vestiges of their shared life slip away like autumn leaves in the wind. The marriage license that once bound them was now just a document gathering dust in a forgotten corner of her heart.

"Enjoy the show, Carl." Her affirmation was more for herself than for him, a declaration of independence wrapped in a simple farewell.

Georgia leaned back, her laughter mingling with Carl's, creating a harmony that somehow encompassed their entire history—its highs and lows. Observing them, April's heart did a curious little dance, a step toward acceptance and peace.

In that shared merriment, an epiphany gently unfolded within her, like the delicate petals of a winter rose. She didn't bear Carl any ill will. Not anymore.

After everything they'd been through, no one would have blamed her for being upset with her ex-husband. He'd put her through enough. But somehow, she'd found room in her heart to push past everything and accept that he was doing something that worked for him.

Even though it hurt her, it made him happy. She wanted that same happiness for herself. Wanted to be free enough to attend whatever festival she wanted. Though her festival would probably look more like sitting in the horse pastures and training them. And less of the dark makeup across the face in the middle of Germany.

No, she didn't wish anything bad on Carl. And if she could reach that serene plateau with him, perhaps she could extend the same grace elsewhere.

Nigel's face floated into her mind, his expressions always so hard to read, like a book with half the pages torn out. He'd been awkward, yes, but malicious? That was harder to reconcile. Despite the evidence pointing toward him, there was an earnestness in his eyes that seemed incapable of deceit.

"Can't believe I'm saying this, but I miss your crazy antics around here," April admitted, the honesty surprising even her. Nigel's situation whispered at the edge of her consciousness, urging her to look closer, to seek the man behind the mystery.

"Trust me, April, it's better experienced from a safe distance," Carl teased, the screen capturing his wide grin, a stark white against the black and gray of his Krampus garb.

"Perhaps you're right," April conceded, the lightness in her tone belying the introspection stirring within. She excused herself from the call with a gentle grace, leaving father and daughter to continue their conversation.

Stepping away, she paused by the window, watching her breath fog up the glass before disappearing—a transient moment of clarity. Nigel might be an enigma wrapped in a chef's apron, but whatever his truths were, she had her own life to lead—one filled with promise, renovations, and the hope of new love.

April pressed a finger to her lips, signaling a soft farewell as Carl's laughter mingled with Georgia's on the phone screen. "I really have to go," she said, her voice lined with a gentle firmness that didn't invite protest. "There's some horses waiting for me."

"Of course, mom. We'll catch up later!" Georgia replied, her green eyes sparkling like flecks of emerald in the glow of the video call.

"Bye, April. Take care of yourself," Carl added, his voice a low timbre that, for a moment, brought back a tide of memories—how it used to resonate through their once-shared home.

"Always do," April responded with a smile that didn't quite reach her eyes, tapping the end call button before slipping the phone into the pocket of her jeans.

She let out a breath she hadn't realized she'd been holding and turned toward the open door. The threshold was a silent guardian between her past and the life she was building, one hammered nail, and sanded floorboard at a time.

The crisp air greeted her as she stepped outside, its bite a welcome jolt to her senses—a reminder of the present tasks at hand. As she made her way across the frost-kissed grass toward the barn, her boots crunched softly beneath her, the sound echoing her determined heartbeat.

Can't dwell, she thought to herself, a mantra to ward off the tendrils of concern for Nigel's enigmatic presence, for the mystery that seemed to cloak him. There was something about him that tugged at her intuition, a puzzle she couldn't help but want to solve—but not now.

Now, there was the horse to think about. The pregnant mare had been an unexpected responsibility, much like the bed and breakfast itself. Yet, they both stood as testaments to April's resilience, her ability to embrace change—and life—in all its unpredictable glory.

"Please let her be all right," she thought, a silent plea to whatever fates watched over expectant mares and headstrong women alike. The barn loomed ahead, a red beacon amidst the frosted landscape, its wooden flanks warm with the promise of shelter and care.

With each step, she shed the weight of past grievances, the echoes of Carl's merriment, and the shadow of Nigel's mystery.

CHAPTER TWENTY SIX

April's laughter mingled with the melodic chaos of her friends' voices, a symphony of mirth that filled the cozy living room.

She sat comfortably, a neatly wrapped box resting on her lap, the paper glinting with tiny golden snowflakes against a frosty blue background. The bright lights from the Christmas tree cast a warm glow over the group, every ornament twinkling like a star in a miniature, festive galaxy.

"Alright, let's get this secret Santa party started!" Kellie declared, her eyes alight with holiday excitement. With an eagerness that matched children on Christmas morning, she reached for the elegantly wrapped package by her feet. "I'll go first, ladies."

The wrapping paper surrendered to Kellie's gentle tugs, revealing a spa set complete with scented lotions and bath bombs that promised relaxation. Each item was a vessel of tranquility amidst the end-of-year frenzy, and Kellie's face lit up at the sight.

"Oh, Beth, it's perfect! I can already feel the stress melting away just looking at these," she sighed, running her fingers over the lavender-infused labels. "I'm assuming it's from you because we've talked about our need for a spa day."

"You know it! Only the best for you," Beth said with a smile that reached her sparkling eyes.

It was Beth's turn next. April found herself subtly shifting in the plush armchair, her palms slightly damp as her gaze landed on the bright red bag.

She tucked a strand of her dark hair behind her ear, a nervous habit.

The projects on the ranch awaited her attention, much like this gift awaited its recipient's approval. She hadn't had much time to shop amidst everything that now consumed her life. April hoped the contents of the red bag would bring joy, not disappointment.

Beth, with a child-like grin, reached for the red bag, her fingers dancing over the soft fabric ribbon that adorned it.

April held her breath, her heart beating hard in her chest. Would Beth find the gift lacking? Or would it serve as a small beacon of thoughtfulness in their treasured circle of friendship?

"Here we go," Beth said, undoing the bow with a delicate pull.

The ribbon fell away like a whisper, and Beth's face lit up as she unfolded the tissue paper cradling her gift. A mug warmer—a simple, compact disc of warmth designed to keep her cherished tea steaming—lay nestled within.

"Oh my gosh, who got me this?" Beth squealed, her eyes gleaming with genuine excitement. The room was filled with the soft glow of Christmas lights, reflecting off her joyful expression.

April's lips curved into a tentative smile. "It was me," she admitted, her voice softer than she intended, revealing the uncertainty that had been nipping at her heels. "I hope it works for you."

"Works? April, it's perfect!" Beth held up the mug warmer, beaming. "You know how much I love my tea during work, and it always gets cold during those endless meetings. This will keep it nice and toasty!"

Hearing the sincerity in Beth's voice, relief washed over April like the gentle waves kissing the shore outside her soon-to-be bed and breakfast. Her heart, which had been perched on the edge of a cliff, now settled back into its rightful place.

She watched as Kellie and Alice nodded their approval, a silent chorus of support in the cozy living room. Their smiles were the kind that stitched the fabric of long-held friendships tighter with each shared memory and gesture of understanding.

With the tension thawed from her shoulders, April reached for the gift in her lap—a parcel wrapped in blue paper dotted with silver snowflakes, tied with a velvet ribbon the color of midnight.

Her fingers worked through the knot, hands steadier now, and she peeled back the layers to reveal a hand-painted journal. Its cover was a canvas of deep blues and greens, reminiscent of the island's summer nights, and it seemed Alice had captured a piece of the serene beauty surrounding them.

"Alice, I know you must have painted this. It's gorgeous," April murmured, tracing the swirls of paint with a finger. It felt like holding a piece of home, a reminder of the new chapter she had bravely begun.

Alice's eyes twinkled with quiet understanding. "For your new adventures," she said, her voice carrying the warmth of a heartfelt hug.

April clutched the journal to her chest, the excitement for her future endeavors reigniting within her. She could already envision herself filling the pages with thoughts from her day, reminders of what needed to be done.

Maybe, just maybe, this would help set her mind at ease.

The corners of Alice's mouth quirked into a smile, her eyes reflecting the joy in April's expression. "I'm so glad you like it," she said, her voice soft but filled with sincerity.

With the moment of warmth lingering in the air, attention shifted to Alice as she reached for her own package, its wrapping paper glimmering under the twinkling lights of the small Christmas tree perched in the corner of the room.

The paper crinkled and tore, revealing a carefully chosen gift from Kellie—a set of artisanal chocolates, each piece a small masterpiece of flavor and design.

"Kellie, these look divine!" Alice exclaimed, her fingers hovering over the delicate gold foil that encased the sweets.

Kellie leaned forward on the plush armchair, a ripple of excitement passing through her. "I remembered you mentioning your love for unique confections," she said, a note of pride threading her words.

Alice lifted one of the chocolates, admiring its intricate patterns before looking up at her friends with a genuine appreciation that went beyond the simple exchange of gifts.

"You all know me so well," she mused, a hint of wonder in her tone.

"Secret Santa was a success!" Kellie declared, a triumphant smile lighting up her face, her arms sweeping through the air as if to embrace the collective spirit of their little gathering.

Indeed, as the evening waned, the laughter and chatter continued, the four friends enveloped in the comfort and camaraderie that had grown in such a short time.

And April, watching the joyful scene unfold, felt a contentment in her heart—a sense that here, in this circle of friendship, she had found a place where new memories could flourish.

CHAPTER TWENTY SEVEN

April's coat whipped about her as she braced against the growing wind, her hair escaping its bun in wild tendrils. The once dormant air of her small island town had birthed a tempest that promised to be more than just an evening nuisance.

She made her way to the barn, the crunching of gravel beneath her boots competing with the howl of the burgeoning storm. The weather was turning; it wasn't just the chill biting at her cheeks, but the sharp sting of sleet that told her winter hadn't yet loosened its grip.

Upon entering the barn, the scent of hay and the warm musk of the animals enveloped her. It was a comforting contrast to the chaos outside. Jackson sat quietly beside the pregnant mare, his silhouette calm and steady amidst the soft rustling of the animals settling for the night.

But as April approached, she noticed his demeanor shift; the relaxed lines of his body coiled into something tenser.

"Feels like it's almost sleeting out there. There's this freezing rain that actually started to hurt," April said, pulling off her gloves and shaking out her dark hair, damp from the unforgiving weather.

Jackson turned to her, and the barn seemed to grow still around them. His light eyes were wide, reflecting a seriousness that cut through any attempt at casual conversation. "April, this baby is coming now."

"Are you joking?" she asked, a nervous laugh trying to edge its way into her voice. But the gravity in Jackson's gaze stopped it short.

He shook his head, short, messy hair doing little to hide his intent expression. "No joke. She's dilating."

April's heart began to race. They had been anticipating this moment, yes, but not under such pressing circumstances. "We need that specialist vet," she murmured, more to herself than to Jackson. With determination fueling her movements, she pulled out her phone, her fingers deft from years of navigating complex legal documents swiftly.

"Good thing Dr. Bennett is coming now then," Jackson remarked, standing now, his height casting a long shadow in the dim light of the barn.

"Let me just call him to let him know he's got to get here as soon as possible." April's voice wavered slightly, but she pressed the phone to her ear, hoping the signal would hold against the storm.

"April? I was just about to call you," came Dr. Bennett's voice, tinged with regret. April's stomach tightened.

"Please tell me you're close," she said, her previous career demanding confidence even when her personal reserves were low.

"I'm sorry, I can't make it in today," he explained.

April's breath fogged the cold air, her heart thudding in her chest as she held the phone away from her ear. The vet's distant voice mingled with the howl of the wind outside, each word like a shard of ice piercing her resolve.

"April, the bridge is closed," came the doctor's urgent tone, barely audible over the storm. "The rain, it's turned to sheets of ice. They're shutting down roads left and right; it's a full-blown ice storm."

Her fingers tightened on the phone, the device suddenly feeling like a lifeline slipping through her grasp. She glanced at Jackson, who was gently stroking the mare's neck, his calm demeanor a stark contrast to the tempest inside her.

"Doctor, she's starting now," April said, her voice laced with urgency. "We can't wait for the weather to clear, this foal has its own schedule."

"Is there anyone with you? Anyone who can help?" the vet asked, practicality cutting through the static.

Just then, the barn door swung open with a groan, admitting a gust of frigid air that bit at their faces. Georgia stepped in, her eyes wide as they took in the scene before her. Without a word, she moved past her mother and into the stall, her hands reaching out to assist Jackson with a confidence that belied her youth.

"Georgia's here," April replied, watching her daughter with a mixture of pride and trepidation. "And Jackson. He's..." Her voice trailed off as she sought reassurance in his light eyes.

Jackson met her gaze, his expression serious but not without hope. "I've been through this once before," he confided, his voice steady. "I don't know much, but I know enough."

"Okay," April said, a shaky exhale betraying her fear, even as she forced strength into her words for the vet. "Jackson has experience. We'll...we'll do our best. I'll call if we need help."

"Keep the mare comfortable, watch for complications, and make sure the foal meets its guidelines after birth. Walking in one hour, feeding within two," the vet instructed, his voice as firm and directive as the icy grip of the storm outside.

"Understood," April said, ending the call. Her mind raced with legal terminology and courtroom tactics, but none of that expertise would help her now. This was about life, raw and real, unfolding in the hay and shadows of her barn.

"Alright, let's get to work," she said, rolling up her sleeves and kneeling beside the mare. The straw crunched beneath her knees, and she could feel the earthy scent of the barn filling her lungs, grounding her.

Jackson nodded, a silent agreement passing between them. They were a team now, joined by necessity and the unpredictable forces of nature. As they worked together, preparing for the imminent arrival of new life, April realized that this storm had brought more than just ice and isolation – it had brought a closeness, a shared purpose with the man she was only beginning to understand.

In the flickering lantern light, as the mare groaned and the wind rattled the barn walls, April found a strength she didn't know she possessed. Tonight, they weren't just waiting out a storm; they were braving it together.

The barn seemed to shudder with each gust of the relentless wind, its timbers groaning like an old ship at sea.

Jackson's figure was hunched over beside the mare, his hands running soothingly along her flanks. The mare's breaths came in labored puffs, visible in the cold air of the barn that had become a makeshift maternity ward.

"April," Jackson's voice carried a weight that anchored her swirling thoughts, "you need to be ready. This foal is going to be here sooner than we think. I'd say we have no more than five hours, probably more like one."

His words hung there, stark and undeniable as the chill that seeped through the walls. April moved closer, her gaze locked onto the mare whose sides quivered with each contraction. She could feel the thrum of her own pulse, the nervous energy converting into something steely and determined.

"Okay, what do we need to do?" Her voice was steady, belying the tightness in her chest.

Jackson's eyes met hers, a flash of reassurance in their light depths. He was calm, collected—qualities that she now clung to like a lifeline. "We're going to do this."

As her fingers brushed against the mare's damp coat, April felt the animal's trust and an unspoken bond formed between them. She noted the way Jackson's presence seemed to soothe the mare, and a realization dawned on her—this quiet man with his gentle touch and steady gaze had layers she was only beginning to uncover.

Her heart raced, not with fear but with focus, the kind that narrows the world to a single point of concentration. She realized that, despite the storm raging outside, this barn had become the center of her universe, the place where life would triumph over the elements.

"Let's hope this little one knows how much love is waiting for it out here," she mused aloud, allowing a small smile to curve her lips.

"Animals have a sense for these things," Jackson replied, his tone soft but certain. "They know when they're in good hands."

And as they settled in to wait, surrounded by the warmth of the animals and the steadfast presence of each other, April felt an unexpected peace. Here, in the heart of the storm, she was exactly where she needed to be.

CHAPTER TWENTY EIGHT

The barn, swathed in the golden light of late afternoon, resonated with a quiet tension that seemed to weave through the very hay and wood. April stood close to the mare, her breath misting in the chilly air as she watched Jackson, whose presence commanded a calm authority amidst the unfolding drama.

"Alright," he said, his voice a soothing timbre against the mare's occasional whinnies. "Our main job is to make sure she's comfortable and safe. We're going to need towels, warm water, and some iodine—just in case we have to intervene with the umbilical cord."

Georgia, her green eyes reflecting a determined spark, nodded briskly. "I'll dash to the house and grab the towels and water." Her wavy locks bounced as she turned on her heel, already heading for the door.

April, her mind momentarily drifting to the courtrooms she'd left behind for this peaceful island existence, felt an echo of the adrenaline those legal battles used to bring. Now it was life, not litigation, that called for her attention. She knew exactly where the iodine was—in the storage cabinet they'd organized near the grain. "I'll get the iodine," she said, moving swiftly toward the barn's feed area.

Rows of neatly labeled supplies greeted her, and her fingers closed around the familiar brown bottle labeled 'Iodine.' Returning to the mare's side, the pungent scent of the stable mingled with a hint of anxiety rising within her. She couldn't help but ask Jackson, "How risky is this going to be?"

"Usually, nature takes its course," Jackson replied, checking the mare's progress with experienced eyes. "If the foal comes out within thirty minutes of active labor, we should be in the clear."

April took a moment to brush her hand along the mare's flank, feeling the coarse hairs and the warmth of the animal's skin under her palm. The gesture was as much for her own comfort as it was for the horse's, offering a silent reassurance that they were there to help.

Her thoughts churned, a mix of worry and hope. The potential for new life here in this barn—something so pure—contrasted sharply with the messy end of her marriage.

Yet, as she watched Jackson, something about his steady demeanor suggested hidden depths beneath his kindness, like the mysterious currents of the ocean surrounding their island. It was compelling, and she found herself drawn to the possibility of exploring more about this ranch that had become her passion.

But those thoughts would have to wait—the mare needed her now. April focused again on the creature before her, whispering words of encouragement, as if the mare could understand her promise to see them both safely through this ordeal.

The barn seemed to hold its breath, the air thick with anticipation. April's gaze followed the beams of moonlight slipping through the cracks in the wooden walls, casting long shadows over the straw-covered floor. She could hear the mare's labored breathing, a rhythmic hush that filled the spaces between her own quickened pulse.

"Got them," Georgia announced, pushing open the barn door with a determined shove, her arms laden with white towels and a steaming bucket of water. Her long, wavy hair fell forward as she set her load down with care.

Jackson nodded his acknowledgment, took a towel from the stack, and dipped it into the warm water, testing the temperature against his wrist.

"Perfect," he murmured, more to himself than anyone else. He then approached the mare with tenderness, gently washing away the sweat and grime from the expectant mother's hindquarters.

April watched, feeling the tension knotting in her stomach as they settled into an uneasy vigil. The waiting was an agony all its own, a silent enemy that mocked her with each tick of the clock she imagined in her head.

"Jackson," she finally broke the silence, her voice barely above a whisper, as if afraid to disturb the quiet intensity of the moment. "How long has it been?"

He glanced at his wristwatch, the motion deliberate and calm. "Twenty minutes of active labor," he said, his light eyes meeting hers—a flash of reassurance in the dimness of the barn.

"Twenty minutes," Georgia echoed, her tone laced with worry as she began pacing near the stall door, the hem of her shirt catching on a protruding nail before she freed it impatiently.

April folded her arms, a shiver running down her spine despite the warmth of the barn. "And what happens if...if the baby doesn't come within thirty minutes?" The question hung heavy in the air, weighted with unspoken fears.

Jackson paused, leaning against the wooden railing of the stall, his posture betraying none of the concern that surely mirrored their own. "Then we call the vet," he said simply. "If needed, he'll guide us through helping the foal out." His gaze shifted back to the mare, his hands resting gently on her swelling belly. "But that's risky. It's not something we want to attempt unless absolutely necessary."

"Risky," April repeated, the word tasting like ash on her tongue. Her thoughts spiraled, considering the gravity of what lay ahead—a life hanging in the balance, dependent on the decisions they would make in the next crucial moments.

Could she carry the weight of that responsibility? Her heart ached with the realization that sometimes, despite the best-laid plans, one had to surrender control to the unknown.

In the quiet of the barn, surrounded by the comforting scents of hay and horse, April felt a strange kinship with the mare. Both stood on the brink of new beginnings, facing the unpredictable nature of life head-on.

And like the mare, April knew she wasn't alone—there was strength to be found in the companionship of those who shared her journey, even if the path ahead was fraught with uncertainty.

The barn was a sanctuary of suspended time, each second blooming longer than the one before as the clock's hands inched toward the half-hour mark.

April's eyes, dark and watchful, were fixed on the mare, her own breaths shallow in empathy. The shadowed corners of the stall seemed to lean in closer, thick with anticipation.

"Mom, look!" Georgia's voice, vibrant with excitement, cut through the hush like the first rays of dawn.

In that eternal moment, life unfurled. A tiny hoof emerged, followed by the glistening crown of a head. April's heart leaped into her throat.

The sight was primal and beautiful, an echo of every birth ever witnessed under the vast sky. She held her breath as nature's miracle played out before them, the tension unwinding from her body as the foal slipped free.

"Welcome, little one," she whispered, the words less a statement and more a prayer of gratitude.

"Good girl, mama," Jackson praised softly, his voice steady and reassuring. He placed his hands, ready to catch the baby as it slowly slid from the mother. The umbilical cord severed without any needed additional help. Everything was perfect.

The little baby had been born.

"Everything's looking good," he announced, glancing up to meet April's relieved gaze. He was the anchor in this storm of emotion, his presence a gentle reminder of strength and competence. "We'll keep an eye on the placenta over the next few hours. But if she stands and eats before the night's over, we're golden."

"Thank you." April's words were simple, imbued with a depth of feeling that needed no further embellishment. She reached out, her hand stroking the mare's flank, a gesture laden with shared understanding. "You did so well," she murmured, her admiration for the creature's quiet fortitude mirroring the respect she felt for herself, having weathered her own storms.

Georgia's enthusiasm bubbled over as she knelt beside Jackson, their collaboration seamless as they gently toweled the newborn. The foal's wet coat shone like polished mahogany under the dim barn lights, her initial stillness giving way to a tremulous attempt at standing.

"Look at her go!" Georgia cheered, her green eyes reflecting a wonder that resonated within April's chest—a testament to new beginnings.

"Strong girl," Jackson noted with a soft chuckle as the foal teetered, then found her legs. Her first wobbly steps were a dance of life, each stride a victory that drew a collective exhalation from the humans who bore witness.

"It's a girl," Jackson said, his glance sweeping inclusively over April and Georgia, making them a part of this intimate moment.

"Let's name her Candy," April suggested, the word springing from a place of whimsy within her. "Christmas Candy, for the sweetness she brings."

The idea settled among them like the perfect piece in a puzzle, fitting, right. Georgia clapped her hands together, delight animating her features. "Christmas Candy," she echoed, the joy in her voice wrapping around them all.

And just like that, amidst the hay and the horses and the heartbeats syncing in silent celebration, Christmas Candy was born into the family.

CHAPTER TWENTY NINE

April awakened to the gentle serenade of carolers from the old clock radio, their voices a harbinger of the joyous day ahead. With a stretch and a contented sigh, she cast aside the quilt that had cocooned her through the night and slipped her feet into the plush slippers that lay waiting by the bedside.

The anticipation of Christmas morning lent a spring to her step as she shuffled toward the lobby of her fledgling bed and breakfast, her fingers instinctively combing through the tangles in her messy, dark hair.

"Ah, coffee," she murmured to herself, the promise of its rich aroma propelling her forward. April filled her mug with the steaming elixir, cradling it between her palms as if it were the warmth of past Christmases, the ones before the divorce, before the move.

She leaned against the cool windowpane, rubbing the last vestiges of sleep from her eyes, and watched as the sun's rays kissed the icy remnants of yesterday's storm, the world outside glistening like a frosted dream.

"Mom! Merry Christmas!" Georgia's voice, vibrant and clear, sliced through the wintry stillness of the house. She still sported her bright red and soft pajamas, similar to April's, but in a different design.

"Georgia, my sweet girl! Merry Christmas to you too!" April replied, turning from the window. Her heart swelled at the sight of her daughter, all grown yet evergreen in her excitement for the holiday.

"Look at this, Mom," Georgia said, pressing her nose against the glass, her breath fogging up a small circle. "It's like the whole island got a makeover just for today."

"Mother Nature's gift to us," April laughed, her own green eyes reflecting the wonder in Georgia's. "No storm today."

"Can we open gifts right away? I've been waiting!" Georgia clapped her hands together, her wavy hair bouncing with each movement.

"Of course, I've been waiting too! I can't keep it a secret any longer!" April set down her coffee and led the way to the tree, its twinkling lights casting a soft glow over the neatly wrapped presents beneath it.

"Here we go," April said, handing a festively adorned package to Georgia. The weight of expectation hung in the air, mingled with the scent of pine and cinnamon, as the paper gave way to reveal the treasures within.

Georgia's fingers, nimble and full of anticipation, made short work of the ribbon on her gift, her cheeks flushed with the warmth of the hearth. Her eyes, mirrors of the verdant spruce outside, sparkled as she unfolded the layers of paper to reveal a soft fabric bundle.

"Ooh, a heated blanket!" she exclaimed, her voice a melodic chime that danced through the room. She hugged the pad to her chest. "Those dorm nights won't stand a chance against this. Thank you, Mom!"

April watched her daughter, the unspoken understanding between them that college life had its comforts and its challenges. As a mother, her every instinct was to provide, to shield, to warm. "I just want you to feel cozy, even when I'm not there to make it so."

She was glad that her first instinct was something that Georgia thought she could use. It was going to be a helpful little luxury. Something that could make the days feel not as stiff and dull.

Next, Georgia unwrapped the small, velvet jewelry box, its contents hidden behind a hinged lid. With a flicker of curiosity, she opened it and gasped softly.

"Mom, it's like yours!" The joy in Georgia's voice resonated deep within April's chest, a harmony of past and present intertwining. "It's perfect."

A sigh of relief came over April. It was exactly the reaction she'd been waiting for. She worried that her daughter wouldn't remember the small jewelry box that matched the one her grandmother had gotten in April when she was around her age.

But it held the same sentiment for them both. And April delighted in finding something as special as it.

"It's your turn to get one," April said, her words wrapping around Georgia like a tender embrace. She sipped her coffee, tasting the bittersweet notes of memories and milestones.

They continued their Christmas ritual, unwrapping gifts amidst laughter and shared glances. Each present was a word in the story of their lives; each smile, a punctuation of joy.

A knock at the door stirred them from their quiet celebration. April set down her mug, its contents still steaming, and crossed the room. "Come in, Jackson! Merry Christmas!"

The door creaked open, revealing Jackson's rugged frame silhouetted against the frosted landscape. His light eyes held a shy sparkle, a testament to his kind nature and the mystery that often shrouded him.

"Morning, ladies. Didn't mean to intrude," he said, stepping inside, the winter chill clinging to his coat.

"Christmas is meant for sharing, Jackson." April's voice was soft but firm, reflecting her lawyerly resolve, tempered by the warmth of the season. "We're glad you're here."

"Wouldn't miss it for the world," he replied with a smile, removing his boots with care.

Georgia beamed from the floor, surrounded by the spoils of morning. "It's not Christmas without friends and family, right?"

"Right," April echoed, her heart opening to the possibility of new traditions, the comfort of old ones, and the gentle hope of what lay ahead.

The aroma of fresh coffee mingled with the scent of pine from the Christmas tree as Georgia stretched her arms above her head, a cascade of wavy hair tumbling down her back. "I'm going to whip up some breakfast," she announced, her green eyes twinkling with festive energy. With a quick kiss on her mother's cheek, she pivoted on her heel and disappeared into the kitchen.

April watched her daughter go, a swell of pride warming her chest. She then turned to Jackson, his presence filling the room like a silent promise of steadfast support.

Extending a neatly wrapped package toward him, she caught the light curiosity in his eyes. "I had a few ideas for you, but then..." April hesitated, her fingers brushing over the paper, "I ended up at the outdoors store and thought you would want something useful."

Jackson's hands took the gift with a gentle reverence. As he peeled away the paper and revealed the small horse bridle inside, his face softened into an appreciative grin. "This is perfect, April. It'll fit Christmas Candy just right."

After debating over all of the personalized gifts at the outdoors store and the engraved knife at the general store, April realized that she didn't need to think so hard about it. She needed to get him something that made sense.

Something he would use every day and be thankful for. It was a simple gesture, the small gift that would come in handy with the new foal. But Jackson was simple, just like she wanted to be.

"Can't have our newest member without proper gear now, can we?" April quipped, the corners of her mouth lifting in shared amusement.

Jackson's chuckle was a low rumble in the quiet room. He handed her a similarly shaped present. "Your turn," he said, the twinkle in his eye betraying his anticipation.

April's fingers trembled slightly as she unwrapped the gift. The reveal of a soft, cozy horse blanket elicited a burst of laughter from her. "We really did think alike, didn't we?"

"Seems like it," Jackson agreed, his gaze lingering on her a moment longer than necessary. "Great minds, April."

The clink of mugs signaled Georgia's return, her hands steady as she offered them each a steaming plate of pancakes. "How about we watch a Christmas movie after breakfast? Something classic and heartwarming?"

"Sounds like a plan." April smiled, her heart full, as she accepted the mug. Her eyes met Jackson's across the rim, and they shared a nod. "A perfect idea indeed."

EPILOGUE

The last echoes of "Silent Night" seemed to linger in the air, a faint memory as April stood before the Christmas tree. It was the day after Christmas, and she was alone with the shimmering lights that now felt like relics of a time already passing, their glow a stark contrast to the dull ache of reality waiting just beyond the festive cocoon of her bed and breakfast.

She could still taste the peppermint from yesterday's hot cocoa on her tongue, but it was quickly being replaced by the bitterness of adult concerns.

She reached out, her fingertips grazing an ornament—a tiny ceramic angel that had been her grandmother's. The texture brought back a surge of nostalgia, but also the realization that the holiday was now a chapter closed. "It’s all over now," she whispered to the empty room, not just speaking of Christmas, but the brief respite it had provided from the lawsuit that threatened to strangle her dreams, the vandalism that marred the fresh paint of her new beginning, and the fake bad reviews that were as icy as the winter chill outside.

Her phone buzzed on the mantel, a stark reminder of the world beyond. A notification glared at her from the screen—another review posted on Christmas Day itself, no less. With a sigh that seemed to carry the weight of her troubles, she picked it up and began to read the scathing words. "Christmas decorations are an eyesore," it began, each word a needle to her pride.

"Of course, they are," she muttered under her breath, a small, sardonic smile tugging at the corners of her mouth.

This review, unlike the others, was almost a badge of honor. It was from the woman who hated the decorations. She'd tried a few times to compromise with the woman.

She'd taken them down for a time, until only two days before the holiday. Still, the woman wasn't happy. It was one thing to be critiqued for something you stood behind, quite another to be slandered without cause.

At least this review was warranted, unlike the several others from people who had never even stayed at the house.

April let out a heavy sigh, the air visibly misting in the cold silence of the room. Her legal mind, once used to dissecting arguments in court, now turned inward, dissecting her own feelings. "I should be upset," she thought, staring at the glittering tree that seemed oblivious to her inner turmoil. "But instead, I feel...vindicated?"

Setting the phone down, she took a step back and surveyed the room—the stockings still hanging by the fireplace, the garlands cascading down the banister, each decoration a testament to her determination to bring joy to her new home. Despite everything, the defamation and damage, she had succeeded, if only for a day.

The other reviews sat there mocking her. But she wasn't going to let it bother her today. That would be a battle for another time.

April stood motionless before the Christmas tree, the pungent scent of pine mingling with the faintest whiff of cinnamon from yesterday's festivities. The holiday had been a warm cocoon, but now the room felt cavernous, the silence a stark contrast to the laughter that had filled it just hours before.

"Hey," came Jackson's voice from behind her, as gentle as the touch of his hands wrapping around her waist. His presence was a balm, a reassurance in the stillness. "You look like you've lost your last friend. Is it just because the holiday cheer is going away?"

She leaned back into the solidity of his embrace, allowing herself a momentary anchor. "I wish it were just that," she murmured, her gaze tracing the outline of an ornament dangling precariously from a lower branch. "It's everything else, all the mess we're in."

"Then let's make our own cheer," Jackson suggested, his breath warm against her ear. "How about another date? We could start a new tradition."

A chuckle escaped her, but it was hollow, bereft of real humor. "And risk Izzy serving up spite with a side of fries?" April shook her head, imagining the scowl on the waitress's face, the malice thinly veiled behind her customer service smile. "Twice is enough for me."

"Izzy?" Jackson's arms tensed around her, and she felt him step back, puzzlement etched into his tone. "Isabell?"

"Goodman, I think." April turned to face him, noting the furrow between his brows. "Blonde hair, always looks like she's stepped out of a fashion magazine, yet works at the diner? My friends said she moved here for a guy."

"Goodman," he repeated, his expression clouding over briefly before he schooled it back into neutrality. She could see the wheels turning behind his light eyes, something clicking into place.

But whatever thoughts were swirling in his head, he kept them tucked behind a careful mask, just one more mystery in a town that seemed to be full of them.

The scent of pine still lingered in the air, mingling with the faint aroma of cinnamon and nutmeg from the kitchen. April stood there, her eyes tracing the delicate glass baubles that adorned the Christmas tree, each one reflecting a fragment of the room, a piece of their recent joy.

But the festive spirit seemed to be dissolving into the cold daylight filtering through the windows.

"Goodman... Isabell Goodman," Jackson murmured, his voice cracking the silence like thin ice. He ran a hand through his messy hair, a gesture of confusion that somehow made him look even more attractive. "April, I—Isabell is an ex of mine. We saw each other for a few months over a year ago."

Eyes widening, April felt her heart skip a beat, not just at the sudden connection but at the raw vulnerability in Jackson's admission. "You dated her?"

He nodded slowly, the sigh he released carrying the weight of untold stories. "Had to end things. It was...complicated."

"Complicated," she echoed, her mind racing as the pieces slotted together with a click that resonated in her chest. Izzy had been serving them both poison-laced glares since April saw her in that diner.

She had come here to get Jackson back. And then saw April sitting beside him at the diner. Is that why she'd been serving her death glances all this time?

"April, I swear I had no idea she'd come to town," Jackson said, his hands finding hers, his touch reassuring despite the chaos swirling around them.

"Of course, you didn't." She forced a smile, though it felt brittle on her lips. "How could we have known?" Bitterness laced her thoughts as she pictured Izzy's golden locks, the spiteful curve of her lips. "No wonder she was doing all of that. Spilling the beer on me, serving us the wrong order, glaring."

"You realize that our exes are working together now." The words seeped out, tainted with discomfort. "We'll have to watch our backs, Jackson. They're playing dirty."

His light eyes met hers, steadfast. "I'm not worried."

"Really? After everything?" Doubt nipped at her resolve.

"Really." His grip tightened gently. "Together, April, we can take on anything. A little extra vigilance, maybe some security cameras, and they won't stand a chance."

"Security cameras," she mused, the idea blossoming into a plan. "I've been putting it off, but it's time to put them up."

"Then let's do it. Let's protect what we've built here." His voice was soft yet carried an unspoken promise, the kind that wrapped around her like a warm blanket.

"Okay," she whispered, allowing herself a moment to lean into his embrace, to feel the strength that coursed through him. Together, they were a force to be reckoned with, and no amount of underhanded tactics would change that.

As they stood there, hands entwined, April knew that the holiday cheer might have faded, but the fight in them was just beginning.

NOW AVAILABLE!

A CHANCE ENGAGEMENT
(The Inn at Dune Island—Book 5)

In this new romantic comedy series by #1 Bestseller Fiona Grace, life gets turned upside down for April Faith when her daughter leaves for college, her corporate job jades her, and her husband abruptly walks out. April realizes she has lived life too long for others, and she needs a major change. She remembers Dune Island, her childhood summer home off the coast of Georgia, a place where nothing could go wrong in the world—and she needs to revisit what remains of her family's historic beach house and see if she can restore it, turn it into an inn, open the door for a new life—and maybe, even, a new love…

"Wow, this book takes off & never stops! I couldn't put it down! Highly recommended for those who love a great mystery with twists, turns, romance, and a long lost family member! I am reading the next book right now!"
--Amazon reviewer (regarding *Murder in the Manor*)

"Wish all books were this good a mystery romance and love. Did not want to stop reading this book—loved it."
--Amazon reviewer (regarding *Murder in the Manor*)

A CHANCE ENGAGEMENT is book #5 in a new romance series by #1 bestselling author Fiona Grace, whose books have received over 10,000 five-star reviews and ratings.

A sweet romance series filled with twists at every turn, THE INN AT DUNE ISLAND will make you laugh and cry as it transports you to a magical place. A page-turner packed with jaw-dropping twists, impossible to put down, it will make you fall in love with romance all over again.

Future books in the series are also available!

"The story line wasn't just a who done it, but had a story about her life and romance, including village life. Very entertaining."
--Amazon reviewer (regarding *Murder in the Manor*)

"It has endearing and sometimes quirky characters, a plot that keeps you reading and the right amount of romance. I can't wait to start book two!"
--Amazon reviewer (regarding *Murder in the Manor*)

"What a great story of murder, romance, new beginnings, love, friend ships and a wonderful cascade of mystery."
--Amazon reviewer (regarding *Murder in the Manor*)

Fiona Grace

Fiona Grace is author of the LACEY DOYLE COZY MYSTERY series, comprising nine books; of the TUSCAN VINEYARD COZY MYSTERY series, comprising seven books; of the DUBIOUS WITCH COZY MYSTERY series, comprising three books; of the BEACHFRONT BAKERY COZY MYSTERY series, comprising six books; of the CATS AND DOGS COZY MYSTERY series, comprising nine books; of the ELIZA MONTAGU COZY MYSTERY series, comprising nine books (and counting); of the ENDLESS HARBOR ROMANTIC COMEDY series, comprising nine books (and counting); of the INN AT DUNE ISLAND ROMANTIC COMEDY series, comprising five books (and counting); of the INN BY THE SEA ROMANTIC COMEDY series, comprising five books (and counting); and of the MAID AND THE MANSION COZY MYSTERY series, comprising five books (and counting).

Fiona would love to hear from you, so please visit www.fionagraceauthor.com to receive free ebooks, hear the latest news, and stay in touch.

BOOKS BY FIONA GRACE

THE MAID AND THE MANSION COZY MYSTERY
A MYSTERIOUS MURDER (Book #1)
A SCANDALOUS DEATH (Book #2)
A MISSING GUEST (Book #3)
AN UNSOLVABLE CRIME (Book #4)
AN IMPOSSIBLE HEIST (Book #5)

INN BY THE SEA ROMANTIC COMEDY
A NEW LOVE (Book #1)
A NEW CHANCE (Book #2)
A NEW HOME (Book #3)
A NEW LIFE (Book #4)
A NEW ME (Book #5)

THE INN AT DUNE ISLAND ROMANTIC COMEDY
A CHANCE LOVE (Book #1)
A CHANCE FALL (Book #2)
A CHANCE ROMANCE (Book #3)
A CHANCE CHRISTMAS (Book #4)
A CHANCE ENGAGEMENT (Book #5)

ENDLESS HARBOR ROMANTIC COMEDY
ALWAYS, WITH YOU (Book #1)
ALWAYS, FOREVER (Book #2)
ALWAYS, PLUS ONE (Book #3)
ALWAYS, TOGETHER (Book #4)
ALWAYS, LIKE THIS (Book #5)
ALWAYS, FATED (Book #6)
ALWAYS, FOR LOVE (Book #7)
ALWAYS, JUST US (Book #8)
ALWAYS, IN LOVE (Book #9)

ELIZA MONTAGU COZY MYSTERY
MURDER AT THE HEDGEROW (Book #1)
A DALLOP OF DEATH (Book #2)
CALAMITY AT THE BALL (Book #3)
A SPEAKEASY DEMISE (Book #4)

A FLAPPER FATALITY (Book #5)
BUMPED BY A DAME (Book #6)
A DOLL'S DEBACLE (Book #7)
A FELLA'S RUIN (Book #8)
A GAL'S OFFING (Book #9)

LACEY DOYLE COZY MYSTERY
MURDER IN THE MANOR (Book#1)
DEATH AND A DOG (Book #2)
CRIME IN THE CAFE (Book #3)
VEXED ON A VISIT (Book #4)
KILLED WITH A KISS (Book #5)
PERISHED BY A PAINTING (Book #6)
SILENCED BY A SPELL (Book #7)
FRAMED BY A FORGERY (Book #8)
CATASTROPHE IN A CLOISTER (Book #9)

TUSCAN VINEYARD COZY MYSTERY
AGED FOR MURDER (Book #1)
AGED FOR DEATH (Book #2)
AGED FOR MAYHEM (Book #3)
AGED FOR SEDUCTION (Book #4)
AGED FOR VENGEANCE (Book #5)
AGED FOR ACRIMONY (Book #6)
AGED FOR MALICE (Book #7)

DUBIOUS WITCH COZY MYSTERY
SKEPTIC IN SALEM: AN EPISODE OF MURDER (Book #1)
SKEPTIC IN SALEM: AN EPISODE OF CRIME (Book #2)
SKEPTIC IN SALEM: AN EPISODE OF DEATH (Book #3)

BEACHFRONT BAKERY COZY MYSTERY
BEACHFRONT BAKERY: A KILLER CUPCAKE (Book #1)
BEACHFRONT BAKERY: A MURDEROUS MACARON (Book #2)
BEACHFRONT BAKERY: A PERILOUS CAKE POP (Book #3)
BEACHFRONT BAKERY: A DEADLY DANISH (Book #4)
BEACHFRONT BAKERY: A TREACHEROUS TART (Book #5)
BEACHFRONT BAKERY: A CALAMITOUS COOKIE (Book #6)

CATS AND DOGS COZY MYSTERY

A VILLA IN SICILY: OLIVE OIL AND MURDER (Book #1)
A VILLA IN SICILY: FIGS AND A CADAVER (Book #2)
A VILLA IN SICILY: VINO AND DEATH (Book #3)
A VILLA IN SICILY: CAPERS AND CALAMITY (Book #4)
A VILLA IN SICILY: ORANGE GROVES AND VENGEANCE (Book #5)
A VILLA IN SICILY: CANNOLI AND A CASUALTY (Book #6)

Made in United States
North Haven, CT
14 March 2024